Other Books by Camilo José Cela
in English Translation

Boxwood
The Hive
Journey to the Alcarria
Mazurka for Two Dead Men
Mrs. Caldwell Speaks to Her Son
Rest Home
San Camilo, 1936
Christ Versus Arizona

Praise for *The Family of Pascual Duarte*

"Cela prefers the weird, the apparently meaningless and the amorphous. The world of his novels has been likened to that of Hieronymus Bosch and Brueghel; he sees man as a prisoner in a forbidding universe where chaos and imperfection always defeat the idealist."—Paul West

"A most memorable book. . . . *The Family of Pascual Duarte* sets its author in place as a contemporary of Céline and Malaparte and a follower of the Spanish picaresque tradition."
—Mildred Adams, *New York Times*

"A lover of crude realism . . . Cela is reminiscent of the Celine of *Journey to the End of the Night*."—*New York Herald Tribune*

"Cela's mastery of Spanish prose and his compassionate understanding of the human character when pushed to appalling extremes of degradation make this one of the simplest, most sorrowful, and unsentimental assertions of the tragic in contemporary fiction."—Christian Science Monitor

Praise for *The Hive*

"*The Hive* is rather abruptly and sketchily represented, it is forceful and it is bald."—Saul Bellow

"A work concerned with the picture of Madrid as a whole, it is reminiscent of Dos Passos. Yet, in this way, the author has managed an attack on Franco Spain and its poverty without one political word."—*Library Journal*

Praise for *Mazurka for Two Dead Men*

"The excellence of *Mazurka for Two Dead Men* should at least serve as a reminder that among the many Spanish-speaking countries, Spain is still a source of powerful literature."
—*New York Times*

Camilo José Cela

THE FAMILY OF PASCUAL DUARTE

A novel

Translation by Anthony Kerrigan

DALKEY ARCHIVE PRESS

Dallas / Rochester

Originally published in Spanish as *La Familia de Pascual Duarte* by Editorial Aldecoa, 1942

First Dalkey Archive edition, 2004

First Dalkey Archive Essentials edition, 2023

Library of Congress Cataloging-in-Publication Data

Cela, Camilo José, 1916-2002.
   [Familia de Pascual Duarte. English]
   The family of Pascual Duarte / Camilo José Cela ; translation by Anthony Kerrigan, p. cm.
   ISBN 1-56478-359-6 (alk. paper)
     I. Kerrigan, Anthony. II. Title.
   PQ6605.E44F313 2004
   863'.62—dc22

                       2003070066

ISBN (pb) 978-1-628975-05-5 | Ebook ISBN: 978-1-628975-30-7

Interior design by Anuj Mathur

Cover design by Justin Childress

www.dalkeyarchive.com

Dallas, TX / Rochester, NY

Printed on permanent/acid-free paper

I dedicate this 13th and definitive edition
of my Pascual Duarte to my enemies, who
have been of such help to me in my career.*

* *La obra completa de Camilo José Cela* (Barcelona, 1962), vol. 1, p. 47.

The Family of Pascual Duarte

PRELIMINARY NOTE BY
THE TRANSCRIBER

I THINK THE time has come to deliver the memoirs of Pascual Duarte to the printer. To have done so before would have perhaps been over-hasty. I did not wish to precipitate their appearance, for all things require their own just time, even the correction of spelling mistakes in a manuscript, and no good can come of an undertaking conceived and carried out at a gallop. To wait any longer would also, as far as I am concerned, be lacking in justification: once begun, a matter should be brought to a conclusion, and the results made known.

I found the pages here transcribed in the middle of 1939 in a pharmacy at Almendralejo (God knows who put them there in the first place!) and from that day to this I have thought about them, brought some order into them, transcribed them, and made them make sense. The original manuscript was almost unreadable, for the writing was rough and the pages were unnumbered and in no consecutive order.

I should like to make it perfectly clear at the outset that the narrative here presented to the curious reader owes nothing to me except its transcription to a readable form. I have not corrected or added a thing, and have preserved Duarte's account in every particular, even to its style. Certain passages, which were too

crude, I have preferred to cut out rather than rewrite; this proce-
dure deprives the reader, of course, of certain small details—but
nothing is lost in not knowing them. The advantage of my clean
cuts is that the reader's gaze need not fall into a mire of repug-
nant intimacies; intimacies, I repeat, more in need of pruning
than of polishing.

The writer of these pages, to my way of thinking, and perhaps
this is my only reason for bringing him into the light of day, is a
model: not a model to be imitated, but to be shunned; a model in
the face of whom we need have no doubts; a model before whom
we can only say:

"Do you see what he does? Well, it's just the opposite of what
he should do."

But let us allow Pascual Duarte himself to speak, for it is he
who has interesting things to tell us.

DUARTE'S LETTER TO THE FIRST RECIPIENT OF HIS MANUSCRIPT

Señor don Joaquín Barrera López
Mérida, Badajoz Province
Extremadura

MY DEAR SIR:

You will excuse me for sending you the long narrative I enclose with this letter, which is also long, considering its purpose, but I send it to you simply because among all the friends of Don Jesús González de la Riva (may God have forgiven him as surely as Don Jesús forgave me) you are the only one whose address I now remember. And I want to be freed of its company, which oppresses me every time I think I could ever have written it. My sending it will also keep me from throwing it into the fire in a moment of despondency—of which God gives me many these days—an act which would only prevent others from learning what I learned too late.

Let me explain myself. I know well enough that the memory of me will be more damned than otherwise, and since I wish to unburden my conscience—as much as that may be possible—by this public confession, which is no small penitence, I decided to tell something of what I remembered of my life. Memory was never my strong point, and I have probably forgotten some things which might even be very interesting. Still, I have set out to recount the events my mind did not erase and my hand did not refuse to put down on paper. There were some things would have made me retch in my soul to relate, and I preferred to remain silent and try to forget them. As soon as I began to write down this account of my life I thought of how there would always be one part of it that I would never be able to comment on, namely, my death (which I pray that God will hasten). I was much puzzled in thinking on this truth, and by the little life remaining to me I swear I was more than once on the point of giving it all up, for it seemed there was no purpose in beginning something I could never end at the right place. I finally thought the best course was to begin and leave the end up to God, whenever He should let go my hand. And thus I have proceeded. Now that I have grown tired of covering hundreds of pieces of paper with my words, I will simply bring this account to a close, leaving it to you to imagine the rest of my life, which should not be very difficult, for it should surely not last much longer nor can much more happen to me within these four walls.

I was very much disturbed, when first I began to write the enclosed account, by the idea that even then there was some-one who knew whether or not I would reach the end of my story, or knew at what point it would suddenly be cut short, if I miscalculated the time left me for the work. The certainty that all my steps necessarily had to follow down paths already chosen for me unnerved me at the time and made me resent-ful. Now that I am closer to the next life, I am more resigned. I trust that God has deigned to grant me His pardon.

I feel a certain sense of relief after writing down all that happened, and there are even moments when my conscience pricks me less.

I trust you will understand what I cannot express in a better fashion because I do not know how. I am heartily sorry now that I took the wrong turning, but I no longer look for forgiveness in this life. What would be the use? It will probably be better if they deal with me as the law demands, for if they did not, it is more than likely I would do again what I have done before. I will not ask for reprieve, for life taught me too much evil and I am too weak to resist my instincts. Let the judgment written in the Book of Heaven be carried out.

Please accept, Don Joaquín, along with this packet of writing, my apology for addressing myself to you, and grant me the pardon I seek, as if I sought it from Don Jesús himself, for your humble servant,

PASCUAL DUARTE

Badajoz Prison, February 15, 1937

EXTRACT FROM THE LAST WILL AND TESTAMENT OF DON JOAQUÍN BARRERA LOPEZ, WHOLLY WRITTEN IN HIS OWN HAND, BEQUEATHING, SINCE HE WAS WITHOUT ISSUE, ALL HIS WORLDLY GOODS TO THE NUNS OF DOMESTIC SERVICE, SISTERS OF CHARITY, THE DAUGHTERS OF MARY IMMACULATE.

FOURTH CLAUSE: I direct that the packet of papers to be found in the drawer of my writing table, tied with twine and marked in red pencil "Pascual Duarte," be consigned to the flames without being read and without any delay whatsoever, as being of a demoralizing nature and contrary to good custom. Nevertheless, if Providence should ordain and so dispose that the aforementioned packet, without the elicit connivance of anyone, escape the flames to which I consign it, for the period of at least eighteen (18) months, I then charge whoever comes upon it to spare it from destruction, accept it as his property and responsibility, and dispose of it in accordance with his own will, provided it is not in disaccord with mine.

Given at Mérida, Province of Badajoz, on the eve of death, the 11th day of May of the year 1937.

To the memory of the distinguished patrician Don Jesús González de la Riva, Count of Torremejía, who, at the moment when the author of this chronicle came to kill him, called him Pascualillo, and smiled.

P. D.

I AM NOT, sir, a bad person, though in all truth I am not lacking in reasons for being one. We are all born naked, and yet, as we begin to grow up, it pleases Destiny to vary us, as if we were made of wax. Then, we are all sent down various paths to the same end: death. Some men are ordered down a path lined with flowers, others are asked to advance along a road sown with thistles and prickly pears. The first gaze about serenely and in the aroma of their joyfulness they smile the smile of the innocent, while the latter writhe under the violent sun of the plain and knit their brows like varmints at bay. There is a world of difference between adorning one's flesh with rouge and eau-de-cologne and doing it with tattoos that later will never wear off . . .

I was born a great many years ago, a good fifty-five at least, in a small village lost in the province of Badajoz. It lay, that village, some two leagues from Almendralejo, squatting athwart a road as empty and endless as a day without bread, as empty and endless—an emptiness and endlessness that you, luckily for you, cannot even imagine—as the days of a man condemned to death.

It was a hot and sunlit village, rich enough in olive trees, and (begging your pardon) hogs, its houses so bright with whitewash that the memory of them still makes me blink, a plaza all paved with cobblestone, and a fine three-spouted fountain in the middle of the plaza. No water had flowed from the three mouths of the fountain for some years before I left the village, and yet it was elegant, and a proud symbol in our eyes; its crest was topped with the figure of a naked boy, and the basin was scalloped around the edges like the shells of the pilgrims from Santiago de Compostela. The town hall stood at one side of the plaza; it was shaped like a cigar box, with a tower in the middle, and a clock in the tower; the face of the clock was as white as the Host raised during Mass, and its hands were stopped forever at nine o'clock, as if the town had no need of its services but only wanted it for decoration.

As was only natural, the village contained good houses and bad, the bad far outnumbering, as is usual, the good. There was one house, two stories high, belonging to Don Jesús, which was a pleasure to see, with its entranceway faced with tile and lined with flowerpots. Don Jesús had always been a strong believer in plants, and I suppose he kept after the housekeeper to watch over the geraniums, the heliotropes, the palms and the mint with the same loving care she might have given children. In any case, the old woman was always walking up and down with a kettle in her hand, watering the pots and pampering them with an attention they must have appreciated, to judge by the look of the shoots, so fresh and green. Don Jesús' house faced the plaza, and yet it was different from all the other houses, not only in its several points of superiority, but also in one aspect where it seemed less than the rest: though its owner was wealthy and did not stint, its front was completely plain, its color was the natural color of the stone, and it was not whitewashed, as even the poorest houses were. Don Jesús must have had his reasons for leaving it that way. A stone shield was carved and fixed in the wall over the door; the carving was said to be of great value; the top part represented the heads of two ancient warriors wearing headpieces decorated with plumes; one warrior looked to the east and the other toward the west, as if they were keeping watch against any threat from either direction.

Behind the plaza, on the same side as the house of Don Jesús, lay the parish church, with its stone bell tower and the bell which was like a hand bell and sounded in a strange way I could never describe, but which I can hear at this moment as if it were clanging around the corner . . .

The bell tower was the same height as the clock tower, and in the summertime, when the storks came to nest, some went to one tower and some to the other, each of them remembering which of the two towers it had used the year before. One little lame stork, which managed to last through two winters, belonged to the church nest, from which it had fallen while still very young, when pursued by a hawk.

My house lay outside the village, a good two hundred paces from the last cluster of houses. It was a cramped one-story house: narrow quarters, befitting my station in life. I came to feel affection for the place, and there were even times when I was proud of it. In actual fact the kitchen was the only room that was really decent; it was the first room as you entered the house, and it was always clean and kept white-washed. True enough, the floor was earthen, but it was so well trodden down and the small paving stones were set in such nice patterns and designs that it was in no way inferior to many other floors where the owner had laid down cement in order to be modern. The hearth was roomy and clear; a shelf ran around the chimneypiece, which was in the semicircular shape of a funnel, and on the shelf we had ornamental crockery, jugs with mottoes painted in blue, and plates with blue and orange drawings. Some of the plates were decorated with a face, others with a flower, others with a name, and others with a fish.

The walls were hung with a variety of objects. A very pretty calendar showed a young girl fanning herself in a boat and beneath her there was a line of letters which seemed like silver dust and read MODESTO RODRÍGUEZ. FINE FOODS FROM

OVERSEAS. MÉRIDA, BADAJOZ PROVINCE. Then there was a portrait of the bullfighter Espartero in his bullfighting costume, in full color. There were three or four photographs, some small and some medium-sized, of various unknown faces; I had always seen them there, and so it never occurred to me to ask who they were. An alarm clock hung on the wall, and, though it isn't much to say for it, the thing always worked perfectly. And there was a scarlet plush pincushion, with a number of pretty little glass-headed pins stuck into it, all the heads of a different color. The furniture in the kitchen was as sparse as it was simple: three chairs, one of which was quite delicate and fine, with curved back and legs and a wicker bottom, and a pinewood table with a drawer of its own, somewhat low for the chairs to slip under, but which served its purpose. It was a nice kitchen: there was plenty of room, and in the summertime, before we had to light the autumn fires, it was cool to sit on the hearthstone at the end of the day with the doors wide open. In the wintertime we were warmed by the fire, and oftentimes, if the embers were well enough tended, they would give off a bit of heat all through the night. We used to watch our shadows on the wall when the small flames were dancing in the grate. They came and went, sometimes slowly and then again in little playful leaps. When I was very young I remember that I was frightened by the shadows; I feel a shiver even now when I think of how afraid I used to be.

The rest of the house scarcely deserves describing, it was so ordinary. We had two other rooms, if they can be called that merely because they were in the form of rooms and were used to live in. And there was a stable, though I wonder, too, why we called it that, since it was in reality empty and deserted and going to rot. One of the rooms eventually served as a bedroom for my wife and me. My father always slept in the other room, until God—or perhaps it was the Devil—wished to carry him

off, and then it stayed empty most of the time, first because
there was no one who would sleep there, and later, when it
could have been used, because the kitchen was always preferred since it was not only lighter but also free from drafts.
My sister, for example, always slept there whenever she came
to visit us. The truth is that the rooms were not very clean or
well built, but neither was there much cause for complaint.
They could be lived in, which is the principal thing, and they
offered protection from the wet winds of Christmastide, and
a refuge—as much as one had a right to expect—from the
asphyxiation in the dry days of the August Virgin.* The stable was in the worst state. It was dark and dank, and its walls
reeked with the same stench of dead beasts as rose from the
ravine in the month of May, when the carcasses down below
began to turn to carrion while the crows swooped to feed . . .

It is a strange thing, but if as a child I was taken out of
range of that stench I felt the anguish of death. I remember
a trip I made to the capital of the province to see about my
military service. I spent the whole damn day wandering about
as if I had lost my bearings, sniffing the wind like a game dog.
When I went to bed back at the inn, I caught a whiff of my
corduroy pants, and that brought me back to my senses. My
blood began to run again and it warmed the heart of me. I
pushed the pillow away and laid my head on the folded pants
and slept like a log that night.

We kept a sorry little burro in the stable, skinny and covered with sores, to help us in the work. When we had a run
of luck—which to tell the truth was not very often—we also
kept a pair of hogs (begging your pardon) or even as many as
three. Behind the house there was a kind of corral, not very
large but which served its purpose, and a well. Eventually I
had to seal off the well because the water became polluted.

---

* The canicular Virgin: Mary's Assumption to Heaven, celebrated August 15.

Beyond the corral ran a stream, sometimes half dry and never very full, always dirty and stinking like a troop of gypsies. Still, sometimes, when I wanted to kill an afternoon, I'd catch some fine eels there. My wife used to say, and despite everything, what she said was humorous enough, that the eels were so fat because they ate the same as Don Jesús—only a day later. When the mood to fish was on me the hours slipped away like shadows, without my noticing them, so that it was always dark by the time I went to pack up my gear. Far off in the distance, like a fat squat turtle, like a coiled snake hugging the ground and afraid to move, Almendralejo lay in the dusk, its lights beginning to flicker.

No one in Almendralejo knew or cared that I had been fishing, that at that moment I was watching the lights in their houses come on, I was guessing what they said and imagining in my mind the subjects of their conversations. The inhabitants of cities live with their backs to the truth, and oftentimes they are not even aware that only a couple of leagues away, in the middle of the plain, a country man may be thinking about them while he packs up his gear, folds his fishing rod and picks up his little wicker basket with its six or seven eels inside.

Still and all I never thought of fishing as much an occupation for men, and I always preferred to devote my spare time to hunting. I had a certain fame in the village for being not altogether a bad hand at it, and, modesty apart, I must say in all sincerity that the man who started the rumor was not mistaken. I had a setter bitch called Chispa, half mongrel and half wild; the two of us got along well together. I used to go with her often in the morning to the pond, a league and a half from the village, toward the Portuguese border. We never came home empty-handed. On the way back, the bitch used to run on ahead and wait for me at the crossroads. There was a round flat rock at that spot, like a low seat, and I remember it as fondly as I remember any person, or really, more fondly than many persons I have known. It was broad and hollowed out, and when I sat down there I could fit my arse (begging your pardon) nicely into the groove, and I felt so comfortable that I hated to leave. I would sit there at the crossroads for a long time, whistling to myself, my gun between my knees, looking at whatever there was to look at and smoking cigarettes. The bitch would sit in front of me, back on her haunches, and gaze at me with her head to one side, from a pair of wide-awake brown eyes. I would talk to her, and she would prick up her ears, as if she were trying to get the full meaning of every word. When I fell silent, she took advantage of the lull to run around chasing grasshoppers, or maybe she would just shift her position a bit. When it was time to leave and I had to start off, for some reason I would always glance back over my shoulder at the stone, as if to bid it goodbye.

One day the stone must have seemed, somehow, so sad at my leaving that I could not fight against the urge to go back again and sit down. The bitch trotted back with me and lay there gazing into my face again. I realize now that her eyes were like those of a priest listening to confession, that she had the look of a confessor, coldly scrutinizing, the eyes of a lynx, the look they say a lynx fixes on you . . . Suddenly a shudder ran through my whole body. It was like an electric current that was trying to discharge itself through my arms and ground itself in the earth. My cigarette had gone out. My gun, a single-barreled piece, was between my knees and I was stroking it. The bitch went on peering at me with a fixed stare, as if she had never seen me before, as if she were on the point of accusing me of something terrible at any moment, and her scrutiny roused the blood in my veins to such a pitch that I knew the moment was near when I would have to give in. It was hot, the heat was stifling, and my eyes began to close under the animal's stare, which was sharp as flint.

I picked up my gun and fired. I reloaded, and fired again. The bitch's blood was dark and sticky and it spread slowly along the dry earth.

M Y CHILDHOOD MEMORIES are not exactly pleasant. My father's name was Esteban Duarte Diniz. He was Portuguese, in his forties when I was a child, tall and huge as a hill. His skin was tanned by the sun and he wore a great black mustache which turned down. They said that when he was younger this splendid handlebar mustache had turned up. But after a stretch in prison, he lost his jaunty air, the force went out of his mustache, and he wore it fallen down into the tomb. I had great respect for him, but even more fear, and whenever I could, I ducked out and tried not to run into him. He was curt and gruff in speech, and brooked no contradiction, a mania I also respected because it was to my advantage to do so. When he got into a rage, which he did more often than need be, he set upon my mother and me and gave us a good drubbing for the least little thing. My mother would do her best to pay him back in kind, to see if she could break his habit, but at my age there was nothing for me but resignation. A child's flesh is such a tender thing!

I never ventured to ask either him or my mother about the time he was locked up, for it seemed to me that it was the better part of prudence to let sleeping dogs lie, especially since they woke up of their own accord more often than was desirable. The truth is that I didn't really need to ask any questions because there are always charitable souls about, even more than average in such a small town, people who couldn't wait to tell everything. He had been put away for running contraband.

Apparently this had been his work for many years, but just as the jug that goes to the fountain too often gets broken at last, and since there is no work without drawbacks, nor shortcut without strain, one fine day, doubtless when he was least expecting it—for self-confidence betrays the brave—the border guards followed him, uncovered the booty, and locked him up. All this must have happened a long time before, for I remembered none of it. Perhaps I was not yet born.

My mother was quite different from my father. She was not at all heavy, though quite tall. In fact, she was long and gaunt, and never looked as if she were well. She had a sallow complexion, sunken cheeks, and looked consumptive, or not far from it. She was also violent-tempered and surly, and grew furious over anything at all. Her mouth was filled with language that only God could forgive, for she used the worst blasphemy every other moment. She was always dressed in the black of mourning, and she was no friend of water. In fact she cared for it so little that if truth be told, in all the years of her life I saw her wash herself only once, when my father called her a drunkard and she tried to prove to him that water didn't frighten her any more than wine. In point of fact, wine did not half displease her, and whenever she got together a few coins, or found some in her husband's vest pockets, she would send me to the tavern to fetch a jug, which she would slip under the bed to keep it out of my father's reach. There was a bit of gray mustache at the corners of her mouth, and she wore the thin and wiry nest of her tangled hair in a small bun on top of her head. Also in the vicinity of her mouth were some visible scars or marks, small rosy holes like buckshot wounds, which were, it seems, the leftovers of some youthful buboes. Sometimes, in the summer, a bit of life stirred in the scars. Their color deepened and they would form festering pinpricks of pus. The fall would wipe them out, and winter would bury them again.

My father and mother didn't get along at all. They had been badly brought up, were endowed with no special virtues, and could not resign themselves to their lot. And their defects, all of them, I inherited, to my misfortune. They were little disposed to think in terms of principles or to put reins on their instincts. So that any circumstance, anything whatever, however small, brought on a storm, which would rage for days, with no end ever in sight. In general I never took either one's side. The truth was that it was all the same to me whether one or the other got thrashed. Sometimes I was glad to see my mother get it, sometimes my father, but I was never asked for my vote either way.

My mother could neither read nor write. My father could, and he made an issue of it and never missed a chance to rub it in at every turn, and often, though it might have nothing to do with the matter in hand, he would call her an ignoramus, a word which cut my mother to the quick, sent her into a towering rage, and made her hiss like a basilisk. Sometimes in the evening my father would come home with a newspaper in his hand and, whether we liked it or not, he would sit us both down in the kitchen and would read us out the news. Next would come the commentaries, and the moment they began I would begin to tremble, for they were always the beginning of a brawl. My mother, by way of starting him off, would say that there was nothing in the paper resembling what he had read out, and that everything he'd said had come out of his head. This view of things would send my father off his rocker. He'd yell like a madman, call her an ignorant witch, and always end up by shouting that if he really did know how to invent such things as were in the paper he would scarcely have thought of marrying the likes of her. Now the battle was joined. She'd call him a hairy ape, and denounce him for a starving Portuguee. He seemed to have been waiting for this

very word to begin pounding her, and when the word came
he'd rip off his belt and chase her around the kitchen until
he was exhausted. At first I used to come in for a few chance
swipes, but after a bit of experience I learned that the only
way not to get wet is to get in out of the rain and so as soon as
I saw things getting bad, I left them to themselves and took
off. It was their funeral!

The truth is that life in my family had little to recommend
it. But since we are not given a choice, but rather destined—
even from before birth—to go some of us one way, some the
other, I did my best to accept my fate, which was the only
way to avoid desperation. When I was very young, which is
the age when one's mind is most manageable, they sent me
to school for a short spell. My father said the struggle for life
was very grim, and that it was necessary to prepare to face up
to it with the only arms useful in the battle, the weapons of
the intellect. He reeled off this advice as if he had learned it by
heart. At such times his voice seemed less gruff, almost veiled,
and it would take on intonations completely new to me . . .
Afterwards, as if repenting of what he had just said, he would
burst into a loud laugh. He always ended up by telling me,
almost affectionately:

"Don't pay me any heed, boy . . . I'm getting old!"

And he'd stay lost in thought for a bit, repeating under his
breath, "I'm getting old! . . . I'm getting old!"

My schooling was of short duration. My father, who had
a violent and bullying temper in some things, as I've shown,
was weak-minded in others. It was plain to see that he exercised his will only in trifling matters, and that, whether from
fear or from some other reason, he rarely took a firm stand
in matters of larger importance. My mother did not want me
in school, and whenever she had the opportunity, and often
even when she had to force the issue, would tell me that it was

no use learning anything if I was never to rise out of poverty anyway. She sowed in a fertile field, for I wasn't a bit amused by the idea of attending classes. Between the two of us, and with the help of a little time, we finally convinced my father, who cast the deciding vote in favor of my giving up my studies. I had already learned how to read and write, and how to add and subtract, so that in reality I had enough knowledge to take care of myself. I was twelve when I quit school. But I'd better not go so fast in my story, for all things want their order, and no matter how early one gets up, dawn doesn't come any sooner.

I was still very young when my sister Rosario was born. My memory of that time is confused and vague, and so I don't know how faithfully my recollection will be but I will try to relate what happened, nevertheless, for even if my narrative comes out rather uncertainly, it will still be closer to reality than anything your imagination or your guesswork could produce for itself. I remember that it was hot the afternoon Rosario was born. A day in midsummer. The fields were parched and still and the crickets seemed bent on cutting the earth's bones with their rasping saws. Men and beasts were in out of the heat, and the sun, up there in the sky, lord and master of everything, was throwing light on everything, burning everything . . . My mother's childbed labor was always very difficult and painful. She was half barren and a bit withered and the pain in her was superior to her strength. Since the poor woman had never been a model of virtue or of dignity, and had not learned to suffer in silence, even as I had, she resolved all questions by screaming. She had been howling for several hours when Rosario was born. To make matters worse, she always had a slow delivery. As the proverb has it: A mustached woman who's slow to bear . . . (I don't give the second part, out of respect for the high person to whom these pages are addressed.) My mother was attended by a midwife from the village, Señora Engracia, from the Hill, who specialized in births and burials. She was something of a witch, full of mystery, and she had brought along some concoctions which she applied to my mother's belly to ease the pain. But since my mother, with or without concoctions on her belly, went on howling her lungs out, Señora Engracia could think of nothing better than to call her an unbeliever and a bad Christian. Just then my mother's howls rose to the proportions of a tempest, and I began to wonder if she really wasn't bedeviled after all. But I was not left wondering long, for it soon became apparent that the gale of screams had been caused by the coming forth of my new sister.

My father had been pacing about the kitchen in great strides for some time. As soon as Rosario was born, he came up to my mother's bed and, without the least regard for her situation, began to call her a hussy and a slut and to slash at her with the buckle-end of his belt with such violence that to this day I am surprised he did not finish her off then and there. Then he marched out and was gone for two days. When he did come home, he was drunk as a skunk. He staggered to my mother's bed and kissed her. She let him kiss her. Then he made for the stable to sleep it off.

THEY FIXED UP a makeshift bed for Rosario by spreading a pillowful of thick wool in the shallow bottom of a box, and there they kept her, beside my mother's bedside, bound up in strips of cotton and so covered up that I often wondered if they wouldn't finally smother her. I don't know why, but until then I had imagined all babies to be as white as milk. So that I remember the bad impression my little sister made on me when I saw she was sticky all over and red as a boiled crab. She had some thin fuzz on the top of her head, like a starling or a young pigeon in the nest, which she lost in a few months, and her hands were like thin little claws, so transparent that it made one shiver to see them. When, three or four days after having been born they unwound the cotton bands so as to clean her up a bit, I was able to see what the little creature was really like, and I can say, almost, that she did not seem as repulsive as the first time. Her high color had faded, and her eyes— which were still not open—seemed to want to move their lids. Even her hands seemed to have relaxed. Señora Engracia gave her a good cleaning with rosemary water. Whatever else she might have been, Señora Engracia was certainly a friend to the distressed. She bound the child up again in the least filthy bands, putting aside the dirtiest to wash. The little creature was so happy she fell asleep, and she slept so long at one stretch no one would have guessed there was a newborn baby in such a silent house. My father would sit on the floor beside the small box, and the hours would pass as he watched his daughter, with the face of a lover, as Señora Engracia said, so that I almost forgot his real nature. He would eventually get up to take a turn around the village, and then, when we were least expecting him back, at an hour we were never used to seeing him, there he was, sitting at the side of the box again, his face gone soft and tender and his look become so meek that anyone who might have seen him would have thought, if they didn't know him already, that he was one of the Three Wise Men of the East in front of the manger.

Rosario grew up among us, sickly and thin—there was little enough life to suck from my mother's empty breasts!—and her first years were so hard that she was more than once on the point of taking leave of us all. My father went around out of sorts as he saw the little creature did not flourish, and, since he resolved all problems by pouring more wine down his gullet, my mother and I were forced to live through a bad spell, so bad that we longed for the old days, which at the time had seemed like the bottom, before we had known that there could be worse. How mysterious the ways of mortal man, who abominates what he has and later looks back in nostalgia! My mother, who had sunken into a state of health even worse than before giving birth, received some spectacular thrashings. Though it was not an easy matter for the old man to catch me, he would deliver himself of some great absent-minded kicks whenever we ran into each other, and more than once he brought the blood to my behind (begging your pardon), or left my ribs as marked as if he had used a branding iron on them.

Gradually the baby girl got fatter and stronger, nourished by some red wine broths which had been recommended to my mother. Rosario was by nature lively, and the mere passing of time helped. Though she did take longer than ordinary in learning to walk, she burst into speech at a tender age, and talked such fine talk she had us all bewitched.

The period when the child is the same day after day soon passed. Rosario grew, she became almost a maiden, you might say, and when we came to take notice we saw she was quicker and slyer than a lizard. As no one in our family had ever shown a tendency to use their brains for the purpose for which they were intended, the girl was soon Queen of the May and had us walking around with our backs straight as boards. If her natural bent had been that way, she might have accomplished something decent or worthwhile, but since obviously God did not wish any of us to be distinguished by good deeds, she set her feet on other pathways and it soon became clear to us that if she was no fool it was too bad she was not. She served for all purposes—none of them good. She was as offhand and nimble a thief as an old gypsy woman. She took a liking for liquor at an early age. She acted as go-between in the old woman's flings. And so, since no one bothered to straighten her out, or to use her cleverness in a good cause, she went from bad to worse. Until, one day, when the girl was fourteen, she made off with the few objects of value we had about our shack and headed for Trujillo, to La Elvira's house. You can imagine the reaction to Rosario's flight at home. My father blamed my mother, my mother blamed my father . . . Rosario's absence made itself felt most of all by the increased number of brawls in which my father indulged himself. Before, when she was around he carried on behind her back. Now, when she was nowhere about, any hour and place at all struck him as being just right to stage a riot. It was curious that my father, a pig-headed brute second to none, should have paid any attention to only this young girl. One look from Rosario was enough to quiet him down, and on more than one occasion a good round of drubbings was avoided because of her mere presence. Who would ever have guessed that such a beast could have been tamed by such a slip of a girl!

She was away in Trujillo about five months. At the end
of it, she came home with a fever, and more dead than alive.
For nearly a year she lay in bed. The fever, of a malign nature,
brought her so close to the tomb that my father insisted—for
though he might be a drunk and a brawler, he was also an
Old Christian: no convert he, but a solid-gold Catholic—he
insisted she be given the last rites and prepared for the even-
tuality of making the last voyage. Like all ills, hers had its
ups and downs. The days in which she seemed to revive were
followed by nights in which we were sure she was going. My
parents were sunk in gloom, and of all those sad early days
of my life the only peaceful recollection I have is of those
months, which passed without the sound of blows resounding
between our walls. That's how preoccupied the old folks were!

The neighboring women all stuck their oars in and prescribed their favorite herbs. But we set more store by Señora
Engracia, and it was with her we took counsel to cure Rosario.
The treatment she ordered was complicated enough, God
knows, but since we all put our hearts and souls into the cure,
it seems to have worked, for although a slow process, she was
soon showing signs of improvement. The old proverb was
right: you can't kill a weed (though I don't mean to imply that
Rosario was altogether a weed, neither would I put my hand in
the fire to prove that she was altogether a flowering herb). And
so as soon as the brew prescribed by Señora Engracia began
to work, we could sit back and just let time pass. For she
recovered her health, and with it, all her jaunty exuberance.

She was no sooner well again, and happiness momentarily
visited on our parents—who were united only in their com-
mon concern for the girl—when the vixen again outfoxed us.
She scooped up the skimpy savings at hand and, without more
ado or so much as a curtsy, took French leave, this time to
Almendralejo, where she repaired to the house kept by Nieves

La Madrileña. The truth is—or so I think, at least—that there is always a trace of good even in the worst scoundrel, male or female, for Rosario did not altogether wipe us from her memory. From time to time, on the Saint's Day of one of us or at Christmastime, she would send us a little something in the way of money, which kept us as well as a belt keeps a well-fed belly. But the gesture was meritorious, for she was certainly not swimming in wealth, though she might have to look as if she were, given her need to dress for her gaudy trade. In Almendralejo she was to meet the man who would work her ruin, not the ruin of her honor, which must have been good and ruined by that time, but of her pocketbook. Having lost the former, the latter was the only thing she needed to watch. The individual in question bore the name of Paco López, alias "Stretch."* There is no denying that he cut a handsome figure, though his look was not altogether straightforward, since he had one glass eye in place of a real one he had lost in God knows what tussle, and thus his gaze wavered. The wild look in his eye would have unnerved the toughest bully. He was tall, a regular goldilocks, straight as a willow, and he walked so erect that the person who first called him "Stretch" was certainly inspired. His face was his only fortune. Since women were so mesmerized that they maintained him, he preferred not to work. I take a dim view of this probably only because I could never get along like that. According to rumor, he had been a novice bullfighter in the bull rings of Andalusia. I don't know whether I believe that, for he struck me as a man who was brave only with women. But since these creatures, my sister among them, believed it firmly, he led the grand life, for you know yourself the way women idolize bullfighters.

I ran into him once, when I was out hunting partridge,

---

* "*El Estirao*," from *estirado*: stretched: stuck-up, presumptious, "hotshot."

skirting about "Los Jarales"—Don Jesús' estate. He had come
out from Almendralejo to get some air, walking a little way
into the woods. He was all dressed up, in a coffee-colored suit,
a cap on his head and a wicker cane in his hand. We greeted
each other, and he, the sly dog, noticing that I did not ask
after my sister, tried to draw me out, so he could get in a few
barks. I put him off, and he must have been aware that I was
backing down. Without further ado, and like a man forced
to do something disagreeable, he cut loose on me just as we
were saying goodbye.

"How is Rosario?"

"You ought to know . . ."

"Me?"

"Man, if you don't, then nobody does."

"Why should I know how she is?"

He spoke so seriously that anyone would have said that he
had never told a lie in his life. It annoyed me to talk to him
about Rosario. I couldn't help it. You know how it is.

He kept hitting the beds of thyme underfoot with his stick.

"All right, then. You might as well know. She's good, see?
Didn't you want to know *that*?"

"Look, Stretch, listen here. I'm not one to take much, and
I don't waste time on words. Don't get me started! Don't get
me into a rage!"

"Get you into a rage? How can I, when you haven't got
any rage at all about you? Now what would you like to know
about Rosario? What has she got to do with you? So she *is*
your sister. But she's my girl, if it comes to that."

He had got around me with words, he had beat me at
talk, but if we had come to grips I swear to you by the souls
of my dead I would have killed him before he could have laid
a hand on me. I was anxious to cool off, for I knew my own
character, and besides it wasn't right for me to start when I
had a shotgun in my hand and he had only a stick.

"Look, Stretch, the best thing to do is to shut up, both of us! So she's your girl. Well, let her be what she wants. What's that to me?"

Stretch was laughing. He seemed to want a fight.

"You know what I say to you?"

"What?"

"That if you had had my sister I would have killed you."

God knows that my keeping quiet that day cost me my health. But, I didn't want to hit him. I don't know why. I was surprised he talked to me that way. In the village no one would have dared say half so much.

"And if I find you following me around again, I'll kill you in the bull ring on market day."

"Big talk!"

"Stick you with a sword right between the horns!"

"Look, Stretch! . . . Look, Stretch! . . ."

* * *

A thorn that day was stuck in my side and it's still sticking there.

Why I didn't tear it out at the time is something I don't understand to this day. Some while later, when Rosario came home to recover from another bout of fever, she told me what followed these words. When Stretch went to see his girl that night at La Nieves' house, he called her outside.

"Do you know you've got a brother who isn't even a man?"

. . .

"And who runs and hides like a rabbit when it hears voices?"

My sister tried to defend me, but it was no use. That fellow had won the day. He had beaten me, the only battle I ever lost because I didn't keep to my own ground, and talked instead of fought.

"Look, dove . . . Let's talk about something else. What have you got for me?"

"Eight pesetas."

"Is that all?"

"That's all. What do you expect? It's a bad time . . ."

Stretch hit her across the face with his wicker stick until he was tired of the game.

Then . . .

"You know you've got a brother who isn't even a man?"

* * *

My sister asked me to stay in the village for her sake, for her own good.

The thorn in my side felt as if it were being rubbed. Why I didn't tear it out at the time is something I don't understand to this day . . .

YOU WILL KNOW how to forgive me the lack of order in this narrative. Following the footsteps of the people involved rather than the order of events, I jump from beginning to end and from the end back to the beginning. Like a grasshopper being swatted. But I can't seem to do it any other way. I tell the story as it comes to me and don't stop to make a novel of it. It probably wouldn't come out at all if I did that. And besides I'd run the risk of talking and talking only to get out of breath all of a sudden and be brought up short with no hope of getting started again.

The years passed over our heads as they do over all the world. Life in our house went down the same drains as always, and unless I were to make things up, there is very little I could mention that you could not imagine for yourself.

Fifteen years after my sister was born, and just when my mother looked most like a scarecrow after all those years, so that we might have expected anything but another child, the old woman swelled up in the belly. God knows who did it. I suspect that she was already involved at the time with Señor Rafael. In any case, we had only to wait the usual length of time to add another member to our family. The birth of poor Mario—for such we were to call our new brother—was more of an accidental and bothersome affair than anything else. For, as if the scandal caused by my mother's giving birth were not enough, and by way of last straw, the whole thing coincided with the death of my father. Looked at in cold blood—and except for the tragic side of it—it would make anyone laugh.

Two days before Mario's appearance, we had locked my father up in a cupboard. A mad dog had given him a bite and, though at first it seemed that he was not going to get rabies, he soon came down with the shakes, and that put us all on guard. Señora Engracia let us in on the fact that one look from a rabid man would cause my mother to abort. Since there was nothing to do for the poor fellow, we got him out of the way with the help of the neighbors. Every ruse and dodge was needed, for he tried to bite us all, and if he had managed to sink his teeth into anyone, they would surely have lost an arm, at least. I still recall those hours with agony and fright . . .

Lord, what a struggle! He roared like a lion, swore he would murder us all, and his eyes flashed such fire that I am sure he would have been as good as his word had God allowed him. Two days, as I said, he had passed in the cupboard, shouting like a maniac all the time, and kicking at the door, so that we had to reinforce it with boards. He made such a ruckus that it is no wonder Mario, beset also by my mother's screams, came into the world in fear and trembling, rather stupefied in fact. My father finally fell silent the following night—which was the day of the Three Kings*—and when we went to get him out, thinking he must be dead, we found him huddled on the floor with such a look of unholy terror on his face that he must have gone straight down into the bowels of Hell.

I was most horrified by the fact that my mother, instead of crying, as I expected, began to laugh. I had no choice but to choke back a couple of tears which had started up when I saw the body, with its bloodshot eyes staring wide, and a purple tongue lolling out of its half-open mouth. When it came time

---

* "El dia de los Reyes": Epiphany, or Twelfth Night. The Spanish "Christmas," as regards gift-giving, commemorating the adoration of the Magi at the manger in Bethlehem.

to bury him, Don Manuel, the village priest, preached me a small sermon as soon as he saw me. I don't much remember what he said. He spoke of the other life, of heaven and hell, of the Virgin Mary, of my father's memory. When it occurred to me to suggest that as far as the memory of my father was concerned, the best thing to do was to forget it altogether, Don Manuel passed his hand over my head and said that Death took men from one kingdom to another and that she grew resentful if we hated what she brought before God for judgment. Well, of course he didn't tell it to me in exactly those words, but in solemn measured phrases, though what he meant was surely not very far from what I've written down here. From that day on, whenever I saw Don Manuel I would salute him and kiss his hand, but then when I got married and my wife told me I looked like a mincing pansy doing such things, I could no longer greet him. Later I learned that Don Manuel had said that I was just like a rose in a dungheap, and God knows I was seized with a fury to throttle him on the instant. Then the urge blew over and, since I am naturally quick to change even when violent, in the end I forgot it. Besides, after thinking it over carefully, I was never very sure of having understood the remark. Like as not Don Manuel had not said any such thing—it doesn't pay to believe everything people tell you. Even if he had said it . . . who knows what he might have meant! Who knows if he meant what I thought he meant!

If little Mario had had any sense or any feeling when he quit this vale of tears, it's certain he would not have gone off very satisfied. He wasn't with us long. It seemed as if he had gotten wind of the sort of family waiting for him and he chose to sacrifice them for the company of the innocents in limbo. God knows he took the right road. How much sorrow he spared himself by sparing himself any more years on earth!

He was not quite ten when he quit our house. If that was little enough time for all the suffering he was to endure, it was more than enough for him to have learned to walk and to talk, neither of which he managed to do. The poor fellow never got beyond dragging himself along the floor as if he were a snake and making some squeaking sounds in his throat and nose as if he were a rat. It was all he ever learned. Form the very first we all saw that the poor wretch, who had been born a halfwit, would die a halfwit. It took him eighteen months to sprout the first tooth in his head, and when he did so it was so far out of place that Señora Engracia, our perpetual savior, had to yank it out with a string, for fear it would stab him in the tongue. At about the same time as the tooth incident—and who knows if because of all the blood he swallowed in the affair?—a measly rash or eruption broke out on his behind (begging your pardon), which began to look flayed and raw as a consequence of his wetting himself with the pus from the sores. When it came time to treat the wounds with vinegar and salt, the little creature cried such bitter tears and wailed so, that the hardest heart would have been moved to tenderness. From time to time he enjoyed a bit of peace, playing with a bottle, which was what most appealed to him, or lying out in the sun, inside the corral or in the street door. And so the kid went along, sometimes better sometimes worse, but a bit easier now, until one day—when the little creature was four—his luck turned, turned against him for good. Though he hadn't done a thing, though he hadn't bothered a soul or tempted God, a hog (begging your pardon), chewed off his ears.

Don Raimundo, the pharmacist, sprinkled him with some yellowish powder, seroformalin it was, for antiseptic purposes. It was terribly sad to see him like that, turned yellow and without ears, so sad that the neighboring women would bring things to console him, a fritter or two on Sundays,

some almonds, some olives in oil, or a bit of sausage . . . Poor
Mario, how he did appreciate these small comforts, his black
eyes glowing. If he had been badly off before, he was much
worse off after the incident of the hog (begging your pardon).
He passed the days and nights howling and crying like a lost
soul. My mother's small store of patience gave out when he
needed it most, and so he spent the months eating whatever
scraps were thrown him, and so filthy that even I, who—why
lie?—never washed too much, was revolted. Whenever a hog
(begging your pardon) came in sight, an event which happened
as many times daily in those parts as one wished it wouldn't,
little brother was seized with a fury which drove him wild. He
screamed even louder than usual, he scurried to get behind
anything at all, and there was a horror in his eyes and face that
was frightful enough to have stopped Satan himself dead in
his tracks if he had come up out of Hell at the moment.

I remember one day—it was a Sunday—when he flew
into one of those fits and went completely wild. In his raging
terror he decided—God knows why—to attack Señor Rafael,
who had come to call. Ever since the death of my father this
friend of my mother's came and went from our place as if he
were on conquered ground. Little brother had the unfortunate inspiration to take a bite out of the old man's leg. He
never should have done it. It was the worst thing he could
have thought of, because the old man gave him a kick with
the other foot, right on one of the scars where his ears had
been, knocked him senseless, and left him like one dead. Little
brother began to seep through his earhole, and I wondered if
he wouldn't seep to death. The old fool laughed as if he had
accomplished a great deed. I felt such loathing for him from
that day on that I would have done him in, by my soul's salvation, the first chance I had, if the Lord himself had not taken
him out of my way.

The little creature lay stretched at full length, and my mother—I can assure you I was taken aback to see how low she acted just then—made no attempt to pick him up. She even laughed, by way of accompanying her friend. God knows I wanted to pick the poor child up off the ground, only I chose not to . . . But if Señor Rafael had called me weak at that moment, by God I would have pulverized him in my mother's face!

I walked into the village to try to forget the incident. On the way I met my sister—who was living at home at the time—and told her what had happened. I saw such hatred flicker in her eyes that it occurred to me then and there that she would make a very bad enemy. For some reason I thought of Stretch, and laughed to myself to think how my sister might some day put on those eyes just for him.

When we came home a good two hours after the incident, Señor Rafael was just taking his leave. Mario still lay thrown down where I had left him, whimpering low, his mouth to the ground and his scar all livid and more awful than a clown in Lent. I thought my sister would raise the roof, but she merely picked him up off the ground and leaned him back against the bread trough. She seemed more beautiful than ever to me that day, with her blue dress the color of the sky, and her air of fierce motherhood, though she was no mother and never would be . . .

When Señor Rafael was gone at last, my mother picked up Mario and cradled him in her lap. She licked his wound all night long, like a bitch licking its pups just after delivery. The kid let himself be loved, and smiled . . . He fell asleep, and on his lips you could still make out the outline of a smile. That night was the only time in his life, surely, that I ever saw him smile . . .

Some time passed without any new mishaps for Mario.

But there is no escape for anyone pursued by Fate, though he hide beneath the very stones, and so the day came when he was missed and nowhere to be found, and finally turned up floating face down in an oil vat. It was Rosario who found him. He was caught in the posture of a thieving owl tipped over by a gust of wind, turned up head over heels down into the vat, his nose stuck in the muck at the bottom. When we lifted him out, a thin trickle of oil poured from his mouth, like a gold thread being unwound from a spool in his belly. His hair, which in life had always been the dim color of ash, shone with such lively luster that one would have thought it had resurrected on his death. Such were the wonders associated with the death of little Mario.

My mother didn't shed a tear over the death of her son either. A woman really has to have a hard heart and dry entrails when she can't even find a few tears to mark her own child's doom. For my part I can say, and I am not ashamed to admit it, that I cried. And so did my sister Rosario. I grew to hate my mother profoundly, and my hate grew so fast that I began to be afraid of myself. A woman who doesn't weep is like a fountain that doesn't flow, worthless. Or like a bird in the sky that doesn't sing—whose wings should drop off, God willing, for plain unmusical varmints have no need for such things!

I have pondered a lot and often, till this day, truth to tell, on the reason I came to lose first my respect and then all affection for my mother, and finally to abandon even the formalities as the years went by. I pondered the matter because I wanted to make a clearing in my memory which would allow me to see when it was that she ceased to be a mother for me and became an enemy, a deadly enemy—for there is no deeper hatred than blood hatred, hatred for one's own blood. She became an enemy who aroused all my bile, all my spleen, for nothing is hated with more relish than someone one resembles, until in the end one abominates one's likeness. After much thought, and after coming to no clear conclusion, I can only say I had already lost my respect for her a long time before, when I was unable to find in her any virtue at all worthy of imitation, or gift of God to copy, and I had to be rid of her, get her out of my system, when I saw I had no room in me for so much evil. I took some time to get to hate her, really hate her, for neither love nor hate is a matter of a day, but if I were to date the beginning of my hatred from around the time of Mario's death, I don't think I would be very far off.

We had to dry the little fellow off with strips of lint so that he shouldn't appear all greasy and oily at the Last Judgment, and to dress him up in some percale we found around the house, and a pair of rope-soled sandals which I fetched from the village. We tied a purple ribbon the color of mallow in a bowknot over his Adam's apple, and the little tie looked like a butterfly that had innocently alighted on a corpse. Señor Rafael, who in life had treated the boy in such an unholy manner and now felt moved by charity for the dead, helped us put the coffin together. The man came and went, from one side to the other, as attentive and eager as a bride. First he brought the nails, then a board or two, then a pot of white-lead paint. I began to concentrate all my attention on his cheery bustle, and, without knowing exactly why, either then or now, I got the impression that he was as happy as a lark. He began to repeat, with an absent-minded expression:

"It's God's will! Another little cherub in Heaven! . . ." I was so astonished that even now I don't know how to say all I thought. And he would go on repeating, as if it were a refrain, while he nailed down a board or laid on the paint:

"Another little cherub in Heaven! A new little cherub in Heaven! . . ." His words resounded in me as if I had had a clock in there, a clock about to shatter my ribs . . . a clock that ticked in time with his words as they came out of him slowly and oh-so-carefully, and his eyes, his wet little blue eyes, like those of a snake, looking at me with an attempt at sympathy, while I paid him back with a suffocating hatred that coursed through my blood. I recall those hours with loathing.

"Another little cherub in Heaven! A new little cherub in Heaven!"

The son of his mother! What a fox! Let's talk of something else . . .

To tell the truth, I never knew, perhaps because it never occurred to me to think about it seriously, what the angels might be like. There was a time when I imagined them fair-haired and dressed in flowing blue or rose-colored folds. Later, I thought they might be cloud-colored and more elongated than stalks of wheat. Whatever I thought, I can say for sure that I always imagined them to be altogether different from my brother Mario, and that of course was the reason I looked for something hidden in Señor Rafael's words, some double meaning, something as cunning and sly as might be expected from such a dog.

The boy's funeral, like my father's years ago, was a poor, dreary affair. Only five or six people, no more, fell in line behind the box: Don Manuel, Santiago the altar boy, Lola, three or four old women, and me. Santiago went in front, with the cross, whistling low and kicking stones out of his way. Next came the coffin. Next, Don Manuel with his white vestments over the cassock, like a dressing gown. Next, the old women, weeping and wailing, so that they seemed as if they were all of them the mothers of whatever was on its way to the cemetery in the locked box.

In those days Lola was already halfway to being my girl. I say halfway because the truth was that although we exchanged looks full of longing, I had never gone so far as to court her openly. I was a bit afraid she would turn me down, and, though she was always deliberately putting herself within my reach so as to help me make up my mind, timidity always got the better of me, and the affair kept getting more and more dragged-out. I was nearly thirty, while she, who was a bit younger than my sister Rosario, was twenty-one or twenty-two. She was tall, dark-skinned, black-haired. Her eyes were so deep and dark that it was disturbing to look into them. Her flesh was taut, tight from the health bursting in her, and she was so well developed that a man would have taken her for a young mother. Nevertheless, and before I go on and risk the danger of forgetting it, I want to tell you, by way of sticking to the truth in all things, that she was as whole at that time as on the day she was born and as ignorant of the male as a novice in a convent. I want to stress this point, to avoid giving anyone the wrong idea about her. Whatever she might do later—and only God knows the complete story to the end—that is something between her and her conscience. But in those days she was so far from any idea of vice that I would give my soul to the Devil in an instant if he could show me proof to the contrary. She carried herself with such assurance, with such arrogant strength, that she resembled anything but a poor little country girl. And her crop of hair gathered into a thick braid hanging down her head was so mighty that months later, when I was her lord and master, I used to like to beat it against my cheeks. It was soft and smelled of sunshine and thyme, and of the cold beads of sweet sweat that showed on the down at her temples when she was flushed . . .

To return to what we were saying: the funeral went off well enough. Since the grave was already dug, all we had to do was to lower my brother into it and cover him over. Don Manuel said a few prayers in Latin, and the women knelt by the grave. When Lola went down on her knees she showed the smooth whiteness of her legs above her black stockings, tight as blood sausage. I blush to say what I must, and may God apply the effort it costs me to say it toward the salvation of my soul, for the truth is that at that moment I was glad my brother had died . . . Lola's legs shone like silverplate, the blood pounded in my temples, and my heart seemed ready to burst from my chest.

I did not see Don Manuel or the women leave. I was like a man in a trance, stupefied, and when I began to come to my senses I found myself sitting on the fresh earth above Mario's body. Why I was there, or how long a time had elapsed are two things I'll never know. I remember that the blood was still coursing in my forehead and that my heart was still trying to fly away. The sun was falling. Its last rays were nailed to a sad cypress tree, my only company. It was hot. Tremors were running through my body. I couldn't move. I was transfixed, as spellbound as if a wolf had looked me in the eye.

Lola was standing there. Her breasts rose and fell as she breathed . . .

"Lola! . . ."

"Well, here I am."

"What are you doing here?"

"Nothing in particular. I'm just here . . ."

I got up and took her by the arm.

"What are you doing here?"

"Nothing! Can't you see that? Nothing!"

Lola gave me a terrifying look. Her voice was like a voice from beyond, from beneath the earth, like that of an apparition.

"You're just like your dead brother!"

"Me?"

"Yes, you!"

* * *

The struggle was violent. Flung to earth, held down, she was more beautiful than ever . . . Her breasts rose and fell as she breathed faster and faster . . . I grabbed her by the hair and held her close in the dirt . . . She struggled, slithered . . .

I bit her until blood came, until she was worn out and docile as a young mare . . .

* * *

"Is this what you wanted?"

"Yes!"

Lola smiled up at me with her even teeth . . . Then she stroked my hair.

"You're not like your brother at all! . . . You're a man! . . ."

The words were a deep sound in her throat.

"You're a man . . ."

The earth was soft, I remember it well. Half a dozen red poppies had sprouted for my dead brother: six drops of blood.

"You're not like your brother! You're a man!"

"Do you love me?"

"Yes!"

IT WAS THE will of Heaven that two weeks should elapse since I last wrote anything. During that time, what with questioning and visits from the defense lawyer on the one hand, and being moved to this new place on the other, I didn't have a free minute to pick up my pen. Now, after reading this batch of papers—not too large a pile at that—the most confusing ideas swirl around in my head, surging about in a great tide, so that no matter how I try I can't decide how to begin again. A heap of trouble, that's what this story amounts to, a deal of misfortune, as you will have observed, and there is always the danger that I will lose heart altogether when I get on with the rest of the story, which is even more miserable. I can only marvel at the awful accuracy of my memory in these moments when all the events of my life, none of which can be undone, are being set down as big as they might be on a blackboard. It's funny—and also sad, God knows!—to stop and think that if all this effort of will I'm making these days had been made a few years back, I wouldn't be locked up in this cell writing it all down, but sitting in the sun in the corral or fishing for eels in the creek or chasing rabbits over the hills. I'd be doing any of those things that most people do without thinking. I'd be free, as most men are free, without a thought of being free. I'd have God knows how many more years of life ahead of me, like most men, with no notion about how slow I should spend them . . .

The place they've brought me to now is an improvement.

Through my window I can see a small garden, as well cared for and tidy as a parlor, and beyond it, all the way to the sierra, I can see the plain, as brown as a man's skin. From time to time a line of mules crosses on the way to Portugal; donkeys jog along out to the small houses; and women and children walk by on their way to the well.

I breathe my own air, the free air that comes and goes from my cell, free because they haven't any charges against it; it's the same air that a passing muleteer may breathe tomorrow, or some other day . . . I can see a butterfly, a splash of color, wheeling around the sunflowers. It flutters into the cell, takes a couple of turns around the room, and makes its easy way out, as they've got nothing against it, either. Perhaps it will go on to light on the warden's pillow . . .

I use my cap to catch the mouse nibbling at what I'd left for him. I look at him closely, and then I let him go—I've got no charge to hold him on—and watch him run off in his mincing way into the hole where he hides, and from where he comes to eat the stranger's food, the leftovers of a stranger who stays in the cell only a short time, before he quits the place, most often, to go to Hell.

You would probably not believe me if I were to tell you that such sadness sweeps over me, such melancholy, I almost dare say my repentance is much the same as a saint's. Probably you would not believe me, for the reports you have of me must be pretty bad, and the opinion formed of me by now the same, and yet . . . I tell you what I tell you, perhaps merely for the telling, perhaps merely so as not to give up my fixed idea that you will understand what I tell you and believe the truth of what I do not swear to on my salvation only because there would be little use swearing on that . . . There is such a bitter taste in my throat that I think my heart must pump bile instead of blood. It mounts in my chest and leaves an acid taste under my tongue. It floods my mouth, but dries me up inside, as if it were a foul wind from a cemetery niche.

I stopped writing at this point, for maybe twenty minutes, or an hour, or two . . . Down along the path some people made their way. How clearly I saw them just now! They could not for a moment have thought that I was watching them, they walked so unconcerned. They were a party of two men, a woman, and a little boy. They seemed happy just to be walking along the path. The men must have both been around thirty. The woman was a bit younger. The boy could not have been more than six. He was barefoot, and he was romping along in and out of the bushes like a goat. All he had on was a little shirt that left him bare from the belly down. He would trot on ahead, then stop and throw a stone at some bird he'd flushed from cover. He wasn't at all like little Mario, and yet how he did remind me of my brother!

The woman must have been the mother. She was dark, like all country women, and a kind of joy seemed to run through her whole body so that it made one joyful just to look at her. She was very different from my mother, and yet, why did she make me think of her?

You must forgive me. I can't go on this way. I'm very near to crying . . . A self-respecting man can not let himself be overcome by tears, as if he were a simple woman.

It will be best if I get on with my story. It's sad, of course, but it's even sadder philosophizing about it. And anyway I'm not made to philosophize, I don't have the heart for it. My heart is more like a machine for making blood to be spilt in a knife fight . . .

THE AFFAIR WITH Lola developed just as you would expect. Not five months had passed since the burial of my brother, however, when I was surprised—that's the way things go!—by the news that should have surprised no one.

It was the feast of San Carlos, in the month of November. I had gone to Lola's house, just as I had every day for months. And as always, her mother got up and left. Thinking back on it later, I did find my girl looking a bit peaked and pale, a bit odd, even then. She looked as if she had been crying, as if she were weighed down by some hidden sorrow. Our conversation that day—talk between us had never been exactly free and easy—was stopped dead by the sound of our voices, the way crickets shut up when they hear footsteps, or partridges take flight at the song of a hiker. Every attempt I made to speak got stuck in my throat, which had gone as dry as a white wall.

"Well, don't talk to me if you don't want to," I said.

"But, I do want to."

"Well talk then. Am I stopping you?"

"Pascual!"

"What!"

"Do you know something?"

"No."

"Can't you guess?"

"No."

It makes me laugh now to remember how long it took me to figure it out.

"Pascual!"

"What!"

"I'm pregnant!"

I didn't take it in all at once. I was left speechless by the news, which struck me at first as something that didn't really concern me. It had never occurred to me that something everybody talked about, that something so natural and ordinary could possibly happen. I don't know what I was thinking about.

My ears were burning. They felt red as coals. My eyes smarted, as if I'd gotten soap in them.

A dead silence fell between us. It lasted several minutes. My heartbeat throbbed at my temples. The pulsations were quick and short, like the ticking of a clock. And yet it was some time before I even noticed it.

Lola seemed to be breathing through a flute.

"So you're pregnant?"

"Yes!"

Lola burst into tears. I couldn't think of any way to console her.

"Don't be silly. Some die, others are born . . ."

Perhaps the Lord will spare me some torment in Hell because of my tenderness that afternoon.

"What's so strange about it after all?" I went on. "Your mother was pregnant before you were born . . . And mine, too . . ."

I was making every effort to say something sensible. I couldn't help noticing how shaken Lola was. She looked as if she had been turned inside out.

"It's what always happens," I went on helpfully. "It's a known fact. There's no cause for alarm!"

I studied her waist. There wasn't anything to be seen. She was more beautiful than ever, her color faded to fair and the coil of her hair flowing free.

I went up to her and kissed the side of her face. She was as cold as a corpse. Lola let herself be kissed, with a little smile on her lips like the smile a martyr might have worn in the old days.

"Are you happy?"

"Yes! Very happy!"

Lola spoke to me without smiling any more.

"Do you love me . . . in this condition?"

"Yes, Lola . . . in that condition."

It was true. At that moment, that was just the way I wanted her. Young and with a child in her belly. My child. It began to please me to think of bringing him up and making a good man of him.

"We'll get married, Lola. We'll get our papers in order. We can't leave it at this . . ."

"No . . ."

Lola's voice was like a sigh.

"And I want to show your mother I know how to behave like a man."

"She already knows that . . ."

"She doesn't know!"

By the time it occurred to me to leave it had become dark night.

"Call your mother in."

"My mother?"

"Yes."

"What for?"

"To tell her."

"She already knows."

"She may know it . . . But I want to tell her myself!"

Lola stood up—how tall she was!—and went out. As she went through the kitchen door I wanted her more than ever.

After a bit her mother came in.

"What is it?"

"You can see for yourself."

"You realize the condition you've left her in?"

"I left her in a good condition."

"Good?"

"Yes. Good! She's not underage, is she?"

Her mother kept quiet. I never thought I'd see the day she'd be so quiet.

"I wanted to talk to you."

"About what?"

"About your daughter. I'm going to marry her."

"It's the least you could do. Is your mind made up?"

"Yes, it is."

"And have you thought it all through?"

"Yes, all through."

"In such a short time?"

"There was plenty of time."

"Well, wait a minute then. I'll call her."

The old woman went out and was gone a long time. The two of them must have been arguing it out. When she came back, she had Lola by the hand.

"Look. He wants to get married. Do you want to marry him?"

"Yes."

"Pascual is a good boy. I knew he'd do the right thing . . . Go ahead, give each other a kiss."

"We've kissed already."

"Well kiss again. Go on, let me see you do it."

I walked over and kissed her. I kissed her with all my might. I pressed her against me, not minding her mother standing there watching. And yet, that first kiss given with permission didn't taste half as good as the kisses in the cemetery, so long ago now.

"Can I stay the night?"

"Yes, stay."

"No, Pascual, don't stay. Not yet."

"Nonsense, girl. Let him stay. He's going to be your husband, isn't he?"

I stayed. And spent the night with her.

The next day, very early in the morning, I went over to the parish church. I made my way to the sacristy. Don Manuel was getting ready to say Mass, the Mass he said for Don Jesús González de la Riva and his housekeeper, and two or three other old women. He seemed surprised to see me.

"What brings you around here?"

"Here I am, Don Manuel, come to talk to you."

"Will it take long?"

"Yes, sir."

"Can you wait until after Mass?"

"Yes, sir. There's no hurry about it."

"Well then, wait for me."

Don Manuel opened the door of the sacristy and pointed to a bench in church, a bench like any bench in any church, made of unpainted wood, hard and cold as stone, but a place where sometimes some wonderful moments are possible.

"Sit over there. When you see Don Jesús kneel, you kneel, too. When you see Don Jesús stand up, you stand up. When you see Don Jesús sit down, you sit down, too . . ."

"Yes, sir."

The Mass lasted, like all of them, about half an hour. But that half hour flew by.

When it was over, I went back to the sacristy. Don Manuel was taking off his vestments.

"Go ahead."

"Well, you see it's this way . . . I would like to get married."

"I think that's a good idea, son. A very good idea. That's

why God created men and women, to perpetuate the human species."

"Yes, sir."

"Fine, fine. And who is the girl you want to marry? Is it La Lola?"

"Yes, sir."

"And you've thought about it for some time?"

"No, sir, yesterday . . ."

"Only yesterday?"

"Only yesterday. Yesterday she told me what was up."

"She told you something in particular?"

"Yes."

"She's pregnant?"

"Yes, sir, pregnant."

"Well, then, son, it's best you get married. God will forgive you everything and you will gain consideration even in the sight of men. A child born out of wedlock is a sin and a shame. A child born of parents wed in the Church is a blessing of God. I'll fix up the papers for you. Are you cousins?"

"No, sir."

"All the better. Stop by again in a couple of weeks. I'll have everything ready for you then."

"Yes, sir."

"Where will you be going now?"

"Well, I'm on my way to work."

"Wouldn't you like to make your confession first?"

"Yes . . ."

I made my confession, and felt, afterwards, as free and easy as if I'd taken a bath in hot water.

A LITTLE OVER a month later, on the twelfth of December, the day of Our Lady of Guadalupe, which that year fell on a Wednesday, and after having complied with all the requirements of the law of the Church, Lola and I were married.

I was a bit worried, and went around deep in thought, a bit fearful over the step I was about to take. Getting married is a deadly serious matter. I had moments of weakness and doubt, when it wouldn't have taken much to make me turn tail and leave the whole thing up in the air. If I didn't dare do that it was because it seemed to me it would only raise a storm in another quarter and make a scandal, which wouldn't be any solution to my plight at all. And so I decided to just lie low and let events take their course. Maybe that's the way the sheep think as they are led off to the slaughterhouse. . . . For my part I can say that there were times I thought I'd lose my mind thinking about what was going to happen. Perhaps somehow I'd gotten the scent of my own undoing. The worst of it was that my sense of smell didn't assure me my fate would be any better even if I stayed single.

I spent the bit of savings I had managed to put aside all on the wedding—for it's one thing to get married against your will and another to make the kind of show expected of you—and so, even if not exactly brilliant, it was at least as elegant, if I may say so, as anybody else's. I had some poppies and bunches of flowering rosemary placed about the church, and they made it look inviting and took away the chill of the pine benches and the flagstone floor. Lola was dressed in black, in a close-fitting dress of the best cloth, with a veil of all lace given her by the bridesmaid, and she carried sprigs of orange blossom in her hand. She was so graceful and so taken up with her role that she looked like a very queen. I wore a flashy blue suit with thin red stripes, which I had gone all the way to Badajoz to buy, a satin cap new for the occasion, a silk scarf around my neck, and a long watch chain. We made a handsome couple, I can tell you, in all our youth and carriage! Ah, in those days there were still moments when one seemed to sense that happiness was on the way. And how far off all of it is now!

The best man was young Señor Sebastián, who was Don Raimundo's assistant at the pharmacy, and the bridesmaid was Señora Aurora, sister of Don Manuel, the priest who gave us his blessing and a bit of a sermon which lasted three times as long as the ceremony. It nearly drove me into the ground, but I put up with it because, God knows, I thought it my Christian duty to do so. He talked to us, again, about the perpetuation of the species, and then about Pope Leo XIII. He said something, too, but I don't know what, about Saint Paul and the slaves . . . He really had gone to a lot of bother to prepare his sermon!

As soon as the church service was finished—something I never thought would come to pass—we all went back in a body to my house. Without much in the way of facilities, but with the best will in the world, we had prepared food and drink—enough for everyone to eat and drink their fill—for all the people who came and twice as many again. There was hot chocolate and crullers, almond cake, fig cake, and sponge cake for the women, and glasses of sherry and plates of sliced sausage, blood pudding, olives, and sardines in oil for the men . . . I am aware there were people in the village who criticized me for not having served a proper meal with all the courses. I let them talk. I can assure you of one thing, and that is that it would not have cost me any more to have served a full-course meal. But I didn't feel like doing that for the simple reason that it would have tied me down, when what I wanted to do was get away with my new wife. My conscience is clear as regards having done my duty—and done it well—and that's enough for me. As for the wagging tongues . . . it's best to ignore them!

After having done the honors for my guests, and as soon as I had the chance, I got hold of my wife, set her on the crupper of the mare, which I had harnessed with the trappings lent me by Señor Vicente for just that occasion, and, at a good and gentle pace, for fear of her falling off and hurting herself, I took the road to Mérida, where we were to spend three days, perhaps the three happiest days of my life. We stopped along the way perhaps half a dozen times, by way of a rest, and when I consider it now I am filled with wonder and strange amazement to think of the magic that must have been upon us, to make the two of us give ourselves over to picking daisies to set in each other's hair. Newlyweds, it seems, are suddenly brought back to a state of childhood innocence.

As we came into the city, riding at a smooth and easy trot across the Roman bridge, we had the black luck to have the mare shy on us—at the first sight of the water perhaps—and give such a leap that she kicked an old woman just then passing along and practically knocked her unconscious and came within an inch of pitching her headfirst into the Guadiana River down below. I climbed down at once to go to her aid, for it would not be in the nature of a well-born person to ride on. But I soon got the impression that the only thing wrong with her was that she was a sly one, and resentful to boot, and so I gave her a bit of hush-money—so she wouldn't complain—and a couple of pats on the shoulder, and I went back to join my new wife. Lola was sitting there laughing, and her laughter, you can believe me, made me wince. I don't know whether it wasn't a presentiment, a kind of intuition of what was to come. It's not well to laugh at another's misfortune, take it from a man who has been very unfortunate all his life. God needs neither sticks nor stones to punish the wicked, for, as is well known, whosoever lives by the sword . . . And besides, even if this weren't so, it is never out of place to be kind.

We put up at the Blackbird Tavern, in a large room by the entranceway, to the right as you go in. For the first two days we were so busy with each other we never so much as stepped into the street outside. It was fine in the room. It was a wide high place, with great chestnut beams to hold the roof, shining tile floor, and with a lot of good furniture that was a real pleasure to use. The memory of that room has accompanied me through the years, all through my life, like a faithful friend. The bed was the most lordly that I was ever to see in all my days, with a headboard made of hand-carved walnut and with four wool mattresses . . . What a pleasure to sleep in it! A king's bed could not have been better! Then there was a chest of drawers, tall and bulging out in front like a matron. It had four deep drawers with gilt handles. And there was a wardrobe that reached the ceiling, with a wide plate-glass mirror of the best quality, and two graceful candelabra, both of the same wood, on either side, to put one in a good light. Even the washstand—usually the cheapest thing in a room—was elaborate in that place. Its curved cane legs and its white porcelain basin with a border of painted birds were delightful to look at. Hanging over the bed was a large four-color lithograph of Christ crucified. Beside it on the wall was a tambourine with a colored picture of the Giralda Tower in Seville painted on the parchment and edged with red and yellow tassels. On either side of the tambourine were a pair of castanets. Next was a painting of the Roman Circus there in Mérida. I think it must have been a very good painting, it looked so much like the real thing. There was a clock on top of the chest of drawers, too, and it consisted of a small sphere representing the ball of the world carried on the back of a naked man. Beside it were two Talavera-ware jugs with their blue designs, a bit worn but still preserving the shiny glaze that makes them so attractive. The chairs were six in number, two of them with arms, and all six high-backed, with good strong legs, the bottoms upholstered in soft red plush. I couldn't help but miss them when we got back home, not to mention now that I'm stuck in a place like this. I can still feel them, after all these years!

My wife and I passed hours taking in all this luxury, and, as I said, at first we didn't even step into the street. What did we care what happened outside when there inside we had everything that the rest of the city could not give us?

Believe me, an ill-starred fate is a terrible thing. The happiness of those days began to baffle me, it seemed so complete.

On the third day, a Saturday, we found ourselves face to face with the Pair.* The relatives of the old woman we had sent sprawling must have gotten them on our trail. When the kids in the neighborhood saw the Civil Guard prowling around, they joined forces and the moment we opened the door they set up such a racket that the noise remained with us for a month afterwards. What wicked cruelty does the smell of a prisoner arouse in children? They looked at us as if we were rare specimens, their eyes all lit up, vicious little smiles playing around their mouths, the way they look at a sheep being stabbed at the slaughterhouse (the sheep in whose warm blood they soak their rope-soled shoes to make them last), or at the

---

* The Spanish Civil Guard operates in pairs.

dog with its back broken by a fast cart (the dog they prod with a sharp stick to see if it's still alive), or at the five newborn kittens drowning in the watering-trough (those five kittens which they stone, which they lift out of the water from time to time for sport and to prolong their lives for a while—that's how much they love them!—and to prevent their getting out of their misery too quickly).

The first sight of the Civil Guard gave me quite a shock, and, though I did my best to appear calm, I'm very much afraid that my agitation showed through. There was a third person with the Civil Guard, a young man perhaps twenty-five years old, the old woman's grandson, lanky and cocky as men are at his age. And that was my salvation, that he was the way he was, for as you know yourself, the best way to deal with such people is to use fine words and jingle some silver. And so, I no sooner called him a good sport and a fine figure of a man, and slipped six pesetas into the palm of his hand, than he made off in a flash, happy as a lark. I'm sure he asked God for the favor of seeing his grandmother under the hooves of a horse a few more times in this life. The Civil Guard, perhaps because the offended party saw the light so quickly, stroked their mustaches, cleared their throats, spoke of the danger of a quick spur, and then—and that was what counted—went away without badgering me any further.

Lola was numb with fear from the visit. But she was no coward, merely a bit easy to take fright, and so she was soon herself again, the color back in her cheeks, the sparkle in her eyes, and the little smile on her lips—as splendid a piece of womanhood as ever.

It was then—I remember it perfectly—that I noticed something irregular about her belly, and I felt a pang in my heart to see her like that. In the midst of all my confusion, this feeling served to quiet my conscience, for I had been a bit worried over my coldness at the idea of a firstborn child. There really wasn't much to see, though, and if I hadn't already known, I suppose I wouldn't have noticed anything.

We bought a few things for the house in Mérida, but since we didn't have much money with us, and I had cut into what we had by giving the six pesetas to the old woman's grandson, I decided to return home to the village at once. It didn't strike me that a prudent man should empty his purse to the very last coin. I saddled the mare once again, harnessed her with the fair-day trappings lent me by Señor Vicente, rolled my blanket up behind the saddletree, and thus returned to Torremejía, with my wife riding behind me, just as we'd come. Since my house was situated, as you will remember, on the Almendralejo road, and since we were coming from Mérida, we had to ride through the town, past every doorway in the place. Everybody in town—it was late afternoon and everyone was back from the fields—saw us coming, in all our glory, and they welcomed us warmly, for at that time they held us in high esteem. I dismounted, going over the horse's head so as not to kick Lola in the process, and found myself surrounded and hailed by the friends of my bachelor days and my fellow fieldworkers. They carried me off, almost in the air, to the tavern run by Martinete, "El Gallo,"—"The Cock." We burst in like an avalanche, all singing, and the owner hugged me to his paunch, where I almost suffocated in his giant embrace and in the reek of white wine he gave off. I kissed Lola on the cheek and sent her home to greet her friends and wait for me. She went off, lovely rider on a lovely mare, as haughty and upright as an infanta, all unknowing—as always happens— that the animal would be the cause of the first disaster in our life together.

There was a guitar in the tavern, and plenty of wine and great good humor and we were soon in a high state of radiant excitement, taken up with ourselves, far from the world. Between the song and the drink and the talk, time slipped away. Zacarías, from Don Julián's place, started singing *seguidillas*, and it was a pleasure to listen to him, for he had a voice as sweet as a linnet's. While he sang we all kept quiet, as dumb as mutes—at least we did at first, while we were still sober. But then when we got heated with the wine we all began to sing in turn, and though our voices were not exactly tuneful, we amused each other and everything was fine.

It's too bad we never know where our high spirits are leading us, for we would surely be able to save ourselves some grief if we did. I say this simply because none of us knew when to stop that night at El Gallo's tavern. And so the outcome of it all was total disorder. What happened was very simple, as simple as everything else that complicates our life.

Fish get in trouble from opening their mouths, as they say, and whoever talks much errs much, and a shut mouth swallows no flies, and in truth there's a lot in what they say, for if Zacarías had kept quiet, as God meant him to, and had not gone too far, he would have saved himself some trouble and he wouldn't now be used by his neighbors to tell when rain is coming because of his three scars. Wine is not a wise counselor.

In the middle of the din, Zacarías tried to be funny and told a tale about something that happened, or was supposed to have happened, I don't know which, involving a wife-stealer. I would have sworn then—and I would go on maintaining it right now—that what he said was a reflection on me. I was never the touchy one, heaven knows, but there are some things which are so pointed—or seem so pointed—that there is no way to avoid taking offense, or to keep one's temper and pretend not to notice.

I called him to order.

"I'm damned if I see the joke!"

"Well everyone else does, Pascual."

"That may be, and I don't deny it. But what I say is, it isn't right to make everyone laugh by taking advantage of another man."

"You don't need to put the shoe on, Pascual. You know the saying, if the shoe fits . . ."

"And I also don't think a man should answer insults with jokes."

"You can't be referring to me . . ."

"No, I'm referring to the governor."

"Well, I don't think you're enough of a man to be making so much trouble."

"I'm as good as my word."

"Your word?"

"Yes!"

I stood up.

"Do you want to go out into the field?"

"No need to!"

"You're feeling pretty brave!"

The friends made way. It's never been a man's business to try to stop the knives from flashing.

Slowly and deliberately I unclasped my knife. At such a time, a hasty move, the smallest slip, can lead to fatal consequences. It had grown so quiet in the tavern you could have heard a fly buzz.

I went for him, and, without giving him time to straighten out, I got in the three slashes that left him all atremble. When they carried him off to Don Raimundo's pharmacy the blood was flowing from him like water from a spring . . .

I STRUCK OUT for home, accompanied by three or four close friends, pretty miserable because of what had happened.

"That was a bad break . . . and just three days married."

We walked along in silence, hanging our heads, bowed down.

"He was looking for it. My conscience is clear as a bell. Why didn't he keep his mouth shut!"

"Don't go on about it, Pascual."

"Man, it's only that I'm a little bit sorry. Now that it's all over!"

Dawn was breaking and the crowing roosters were announcing it on the wind. The fields smelled of rock-roses and thyme.

"Where did I cut him?"

"In the shoulder."

'Was it bad?"

"Three cuts."

"Will he pull through?"

"Man, I suppose so! I think he'll pull through!"

"It's better if he does."

My house never seemed so far away as on that night.

"It's cold . . ."

"I don't know, I don't feel anything."

"I guess it's just me!"

"It may be . . ."

We were passing by the cemetery.

"It must be awful to be in there!"

"Man! Why do you say that? You get the damnedest ideas!"

"That's the way it is."

The cypress looked like a tall dry ghost, a sentinel standing guard over the dead . . .

"That's an ugly tree, that tree . . ."

"Very ugly."

There was an owl in the cypress tree, a bird of ill omen, and he hooted mysteriously.

"That's an evil bird, that one."

"Very evil."

"And it's there every night."

"Every night . . ."

"As if it liked living among the dead."

"You'd think so . . ."

"What's the matter now?"

"Nothing! Nothing's the matter! Just nerves . . ."

I looked over at Domingo. He was as pale as a man on his deathbed.

"Are you sick?"

"No . . "

"Are you afraid?"

"Afraid? Who would I be afraid of?"

"Of nobody, man, of nobody. It was just something to say."

Señorito Sebastián put in:

"Come on now, be quiet, the two of you. We don't want another row starting up."

"No . . ."

"Is it much farther, Pascual? I can't remember."

"Not much. Why?"

"No reason . . ."

It was as if some mysterious hand had picked up the house and were carrying it farther and farther away.

"Could we have gone by it?"

"No chance. We would have seen some light."

We fell silent again. It could not be much farther.

"Is that it?"

"Yes."

"Why didn't you say so?"

"What for? Didn't you know it?"

I was surprised at the silence that enveloped my house. The womenfolk would surely still be there, as was the custom, and everyone knows how loud women talk.

"They must all be asleep."

"I don't think so. There's a light in there."

We drew closer. Sure enough, there was a light burning.

Señora Engracia was at the door. She pronounced the s at the ends of words so that she sounded like the owl in the cypress tree. The two of them looked alike, too.

"What are you doing here?"

"Why, waiting for you, son."

"Waiting for me?"

"Yes."

I didn't like the mysterious way she spoke to me at all.

"Let me by!"

"Don't go in!"

"Why not?"

"Better not!"

"This is my house!"

"I know that, son. May it be yours for many years more. But you'd better not go in."

"But why shouldn't I go in?"

"You just can't. Your wife is ill!"

"Ill?"

"Yes."

"What's the matter with her?"

"Nothing. Only she aborted."

"Aborted?"

"Yes. The mare threw her . . ."

I saw red. I was suddenly blinded with rage. I could scarcely make out what I heard.

"Where's the mare?"

"In the stable."

The door into the stable from the corral was low. I had to stoop to get through. It was dark as pitch inside.

"*To, yegua!*" I called the mare softly.

The mare sidled up against the wall of the manger. I opened my knife carefully. At such a moment, one false move can have fatal consequences.

"*To, yegua!* Whoa, come up, mare!"

Again the cock crowed in the dawn . . .

"*To, yegua!*"

She was moving toward the corner of the stall. I came closer. Close enough to give her a pat on the flank. The animal was wide awake, restive, impatient . . .

"*To, yegua!* Come up, mare!"

It was a matter of a moment. I hurled myself against her, and stabbed her. I stabbed her at least twenty times . . .

Her skin was hard. Much harder than Zacarías' . . . When I quit the stable my arm was aching. I was covered with blood up to my elbow. The mare hadn't made a sound. She only breathed deeper, and faster, like when we put her to the stud.

I CAN TELL you for a fact—though later, when I cooled off, I was of the opposite opinion—at that moment the only notion I had in my head was that Lola really might have thought of having her miscarriage while she was still single. What a lot of gall, poison and bitterness that would have saved us!

As a consequence of that unfortunate accident I fell into the blackest despair, and twelve long months went by during which I wandered about the village like a lost soul.

A year later, about a year after what would have been our future was brought to naught, Lola got pregnant again. I was relieved to be prey to the same anxieties and forebodings as the first time. Time passed so much more slowly than I wanted it to, and I got into a wild temper. The black mood grew to be like a shadow I couldn't shake off.

I turned sullen and morose, apprehensive and gloomy. Since neither my mother nor my wife wanted to be at all accommodating, we were all constantly on edge and on the verge of a row. The tension was tearing us apart, and yet it seemed as if we were deliberately cultivating our own irritation. We took everything as a personal slight, assumed every move had an evil intent and every word a hidden meaning. You can scarcely imagine the sullenness of those months!

The idea that my wife could even now have another miscarriage drove me out of my mind. My friends noticed I had become rather odd. Even Chispa the dog—still alive then—seemed to look at me with less affection.

I'd talk to her, in the same way as always.

"What's the matter, old girl?"

And she'd look at me as if she were begging for something, wagging her short tail very fast, almost whimpering, with an expression in her eyes that was enough to touch your heart. She too had had her young smothered in her belly. For all her innocence, she may well have suspected how I felt about her misfortune! The little stillborn dogs had been three in number. Three pups all just alike, as sticky as syrup, half mangy and gray as rats. She dug a hole in the middle of a clump of lavender, and there she buried them. Whenever we took to the woods after rabbits and stopped to draw a breath in that area, she would sniff out the hole, on her face the sadness of all females without offspring.

Lola entered her eighth month, and everything was going along as if mounted on rails. Thanks to the advice of Señora Engracia, my wife's pregnancy seemed destined to become a model of its kind. The months behind us and the few weeks left ahead of us seemed to indicate that we could stop worrying now. And yet, I felt every kind of anxiety, and burned with fits of impatience. I became so restless and uneasy, so disturbed, that from that time on I was convinced I would never lose my mind altogether if I didn't then.

About the time indicated by Señora Engracia, and just as if Lola had been a clock—she was that regular—my new son, my firstborn, came into the world. And he arrived so easily and so happily that I was taken completely by surprise, and was still suspicious even then. We baptized him Pascual after his father, your servant. I would like to have named him Eduardo, because he was born on that saint's day, and it was the custom of the countryside. But my wife, who was more affectionate than ever before, insisted on giving the child my name, and it didn't take her long to convince me. For her notion was flattering and pleased me very much. It doesn't seem possible now, but I can assure you that at the time I was as taken with my wife's show of devotion as a boy with a new pair of boots. I was deeply grateful to her, I give you my word.

Since she was by nature strong and vigorous, two days after labor she was new again and acted as if nothing had happened at all. The figure she cut, with her hair down around her naked shoulders giving her breast to the infant, made one of the most beautiful sights I have ever seen. That alone more than made up for the hundreds of bad times past.

I spent long hours sitting at the foot of the bed. Lola, speaking softly, as if awfully shy, would say:

"Now I've given you the first one . . ."

"Yes."

"And a handsome child he is . . ."

"Thank God."

"Now we've got to take good care of him."

"Yes, now's the time we have to be careful."

"Of the hogs . . ."

The memory of my poor brother Mario used to haunt me. If I had a son who suffered like Mario, a son who had his luck and his misfortune, I'd have drowned him to save him from any more suffering.

"Yes, of the hogs . . ."

"And of fevers, too."

"Yes."

"And keep him from getting sunstroke."

"Yes, we have to be careful of sunstroke, too."

The thought of how that tender piece of flesh who was my son would be exposed to such perils gave me gooseflesh.

"We'll have him vaccinated."

"When he's a little older . . ."

"And we'll always put shoes on him, so he doesn't cut his feet."

"And when he's seven little years old, we'll send him to school."

"And I'll teach him to hunt . . ."

Lola would laugh at the end of our conversations. She was so happy! And—why not say so?—I was happy, too. I was happy to see her like that, the fairest of the fair, with a child in her arms just like the Blessed Virgin Mary.

"We'll make a useful man of him!"

How far we were from guessing that God—who disposes of all things for the better order of the universe—was to take him from us! Our dream of happiness, our only property, our entire fortune, our son, we were finally to lose, lose him even before we could get a chance to guide his steps or set him upon any path at all. Mysteries of love, of loves which vanish when we need them most!

Without quite knowing why, my pleasure in watching the child was undermined by some vague foreboding. I always did have an eye for disaster—I don't know whether to my benefit or my detriment. And the presentiment I felt then, like all the others, was confirmed a few months later, as if to round off my ill-luck, an ill-luck never quite rounded off.

My wife kept talking to me about the child.

"He's growing up fine . . . He's like a little butterball."

At last, the never-ending talk and more talk about the little creature began to turn me against him. He was only going to leave us in the lurch, sink us in the depths of the most awful despair, leave us abandoned like those ruined farmhouses which are given over to an undergrowth of briars and brambles, left to the frogs and the lizards, and I knew it already, I sensed it, I was sure of it, I was hypnotized by the fatal inevitability of it, certain that sooner or later it had to happen, and the knowledge that I was powerless to oppose what was coming, to halt what instinct told me was bound to come, stretched my nerves to the breaking point.

There were times when I'd stare at Pascualillo as if I were an imbecile. At any moment at all my eyes would brim with tears. I would find myself talking to him: "Pascual, my son . . ."

And he would gaze back at me with his round eyes, and then he would smile.

Once again my wife would take up the chant. "Pascual, our son's growing up fine."

"That's great, Lola. I hope he goes on that way!"

"Why do you say it like that?"

"You know, children are terribly delicate."

"Don't have such black thoughts!"

"No, they're not black thoughts . . . Only, we have to be very careful!"

"Very."

"And see that he doesn't catch cold."

"That could be the death of him!"

"Children can die of a cold . . ."

"From an ill wind, an evil draft!"

The conversation would slowly die away, bit by bit, as birds do or flowers, as meekly and gently as children die, children struck down by an ill wind, a treacherous and evil draft . . .

"I'm frightened, Pascual."

"Frightened of what?"

"Suppose we should lose him!"

"Be quiet, woman!"

"The little creatures are so delicate, especially at his age."

"Our son is a fine specimen, his flesh pink all over and a smile on him all the time."

"That's true enough, Pascual. I'm a silly fool."

And she would laugh nervously and clutch the boy to her bosom.

"Listen!"

"Yes?"

"What did Carmen's child die of?"

"What difference does that make to you?"

"Pascual, I only wanted to know . . ."

"They say he died of a mucous distemper."

"An ill wind brought it, an evil draft?"

"It seems so."

"Poor Carmen, she was so happy with her child. 'You've got the same face from heaven as your father,' she used to say to the child, do you remember?"

"I remember."

"The more one builds up one's hopes and illusions, the faster they are all torn away . . ."

"Yes, Lola."

"We should know in advance how long each child is going to last us. They should have it written on their foreheads . . ."

"Stop it, Lola!"

"Why?"

"I can't listen to you talk like that any more!"

A blow on the head from a hoe would not have left me more dazed than Lola's words then:

"Did you hear that?"

"What?"

"The window."

"The window?"

"Yes. It creaked as if the wind, as if a draft were trying to get through . . ."

The creaking of the window, moved as it was by the wind, came to be mingled with a moan.

"Is the child asleep?"

"Yes."

"Then he seems to be dreaming."

"I don't hear him."

"And he seems to be whimpering, as if he had something wrong with him . . ."

"More black thoughts."

"God grant you're right. I'd let my eyes be scratched out . . ."

In the bedroom, the child's whimperings grew like the moaning of the oaks when the wind passes through them.

"He's moaning!"

Lola ran to see what was the matter with him. I stayed in the kitchen smoking a cigarette, the same cigarette I'm always smoking when the blow falls.

* * *

He lasted only a few days. When we returned him to the earth, he was eleven months old. Eleven months of life and care and work which an ill wind, a treacherous and evil draft, laid low.

WHO KNOWS IF it were not God's vengeance upon me for all the sins I had committed and all the sins I would still commit! Who knows if it were not written in the divine record that misfortune was my only sign, that the road to disaster was the only path my dogged footsteps could travel throughout all my sad days?

One does not ever get used to misfortune, believe me, for we are always sure the present affliction must be the last, although later, with the passage of time, we begin to be convinced—with what misery of heart!—that the worst is yet to come . . .

I think of these things now, because if I thought I would die of anguish at the time of Lola's miscarriage or the knifing of Zacarías, it was simply because—believe me!—I had no idea of how bad things would get.

There were three women around me when Pascualillo left us, three women to whom I was joined by some tie or other, though at times I felt them to be as strange to me as any passing stranger, as remote from me as was the rest of the world, and not one of these three women, I give you my word, not one of them was capable, either through her tenderness or simply by her manner, of lightening the burden of pain caused by the death of my son. On the contrary, it seemed as if they had come to an agreement to embitter my life. The three were my wife, my mother, and my sister.

Who would have thought this possible, and I putting my

hopes in the company of the three of them!

Women are as ungrateful and mean as jackdaws.

They howled in chorus:

"The little angel, carried off by an ill wind, an evil draft!"

"Taken away from us, taken to limbo!"

"The little creature who was the living image of the sun!"

"Oh, the agony, the death throes!"

"I held him gasping in these arms!"

It sounded like a litany, as slow and weary as a night filled with wine, as languid and heavy as the pace of an ass.

And they went on in this way day after day, week after week . . . It was frightful, dreadful, the curse of God, vengeance from on high.

I controlled myself.

It's love, I reflected, that makes them cruel in spite of themselves.

I tried not to hear, to take no notice, to pay no more attention to their ritual than if they had been puppets, to lend no weight to their words . . . I was letting time take care of my sorrow, letting it fade like a cut rose fades, keeping my peace, packing my sorrow away like a jewel, striving to suffer as little as possible. All vain illusions, these were, and every day I wondered all the more at the good fortune of those born for the easy path, while God bedevilled me with my fantasies.

I grew to fear the sunset as much as fire or rabies. The most painful act of the day was to light the kitchen candle around seven o'clock. Every shadow recalled the dead boy, and so did the flaring and dying away of the flame, every noise in the night, those noises that are scarcely heard but which resound in our ears like hammer-strokes on an anvil.

And there, black as crows in their mourning dress, sat the three women, grown as silent now as death, somber as border-guards. From time to time I'd try to break the ice:

"It's harsh weather we're having."

"Yes . . ."

And we'd all return to our silences.

I'd make another attempt.

"It seems that Señor Gregorio isn't going to sell that mule after all. He must want it for something."

"Yes . . ."

"Have you been down to the river?"

"No . . ."

"To the cemetery?"

"No, not there . . ."

There was nothing to be done with them. I had never shown such patience with anyone before, and I was never to show it again. I pretended not to notice how odd they acted, trying to avoid a scene. But it came to pass all the same, as fatally as sickness or fire, as daybreak or death, because no one was capable of stopping it.

The greatest of men's tragedies seem to come upon us without our having ever dreamed of them, with the stealthy step of a wolf, and prick us like scorpions with their poisonous sting.

I could draw them as well right now as if they were still in front of my eyes, with their bitter smiles, the mean smiles of women gone cold, with a faraway look in their eyes. The seconds passed cruelly by. The words spoken sounded as if they came from ghosts, from apparitions.

"It's a dark night outside."

"Yes, that's obvious . . ."

The owl would already be up in the cypress.

"It was a night like this . . ."

"Yes."

"A bit later . . ."

"Yes."

"The wind was circling in the fields, the evil draft . . ."

* * *

"Lost among the olive trees . . ."
"Yes."
Silence filled the room like the echo of a bell.
"Where can that wind have blown?"

* * *

"That treacherous wind!"
Lola was a long time answering.
"I don't know . . ."
"It must have reached the sea!"
"Striking down children . . ."
A lioness cornered could not have looked more ferocious than my wife did then.
"So that a woman be split wide open like a pomegranate! Give birth so that the wind can carry off what a woman has borne, bad cess to you!"
"If the water trickling drop by drop into the pond could only have drowned that murderous wind!"

The sight of you makes me sick!"

* * *

"Your man-body turns my stomach!"

* * *

"You can't stand the summer sun, nor December cold!"

* * *

"The heat's too much for you, the cold's too much too!"

* * *

"Was it for this my breasts swelled, hard as rocks?"

* * *

"Was it for this my mouth swelled, fresh as a peach?"

* * *

"Is this why I bore you two children, two children of yours who couldn't survive a ride on a horse or a wind in the night?"

* * *

She was gone clean out of her mind, like a woman possessed by every demon in hell, snarling and furious as a wildcat . . . I waited in silence for the great truth: "You're like your brother!"

. . . the stab in the back that my wife took pleasure in driving home . . .

* * *

It's no earthly use quickening your steps when you're surprised by a storm out on the open plain. You get wet all the same, just as wet, and you only wear yourself out. The flashes of lightning are blinding, the sound of the thunder unnerving, and your runaway blood pounds at your temples and throat.

Now it was the other woman's turn:

"If your father could only see what a worm you've become!"

* * *

"Scratch you and you're ready to bleed to death on the ground!"

* * *

"That wife of yours!"

* * *

Did it have to go on? The sun shines for everyone at one time or another. But its light, which blinds albinos, doesn't make a Negro blink.

"That's enough!"

It wasn't for my mother to upbraid me for the sorrow the dead boy had left in my heart, the dead creature who had been a kind of star for me during the eleven months of his life.

I told her so as plainly, as clearly as I could.

"The fire will burn us both, Mother."

"What fire?"

"The fire you're playing with . . ."

My mother made a strange face.

"What are you getting at?"

"The fact that a man can be pretty balky."

"A man like you is good for nothing."

"Or everything!"

She didn't understand. My mother did not understand. She stared at me, spoke to me . . . Oh, if only she hadn't stared at me!

"You see the wolves that go over the mountains, the hawks that circle the clouds, the vipers that wait in the rocks? . . ."

* * *

"A man can be worse than any of them, than all of them put together!"

"Why do you tell me that?"

"No reason at all!"

I thought of telling her:

"Because I will have to kill you!"

But my tongue stuck in my throat.

* * *

And I was left alone with my sister, my disgraced sister, my dishonored sister, my sister who wounded the sight of decent women.

"Did you hear that?"

"Yes."

"I would never have believed it possible!"

"Neither would I . . ."

"I would never have thought I was altogether damned."

"You're not . . ."

The wind had risen in the woods and mountains, the evil wind that had been blowing in the olive groves that night, the wind that reached the sea after laying little creatures low . . . It moaned at the windowsill. Rosario was close to tears.

"Why do you say you're damned?"

"I'm not the one who says it."

* * *

"It's those two women . . ."

The flame in the lamp rose and fell like breathing. The kitchen smelled of acetylene gas, a lovely acrid reek that strikes through the nerves and excites the flesh, that poor condemned flesh of mine just then in great need of any excitement.

My sister was looking very pale. The life she led left its cruel mark under her eyes. I loved her tenderly, with the same tenderness with which she loved me.

"Rosario, sister . . ."

"Pascual . . ."

"It's a sad time ahead for us."

"Everything will come out all right . . ."

"Please God!"

My mother spoke again.

"I don't see much chance of that."

And my wife, vicious as a snake, smiled through her bitterness.

"It's a sad sight to see people waiting for God to set things right!"

God is in the highest heights, and He is like an eagle in His gaze, and no least thing escapes Him.

"What if God does set things right!"

"He doesn't love us that much . . ."

* * *

A man kills without thinking. Sometimes, even without wanting to. A man hates, hates profoundly, ferociously, and he unclasps a knife. Carrying it open and heavy he goes in bare feet toward the bed where his enemy sleeps. It's night, but the light of the moon comes spilling through the window, and he can see what he's doing. There's a corpse on the bed, someone who's going to be a corpse. The intruder looks at it, hears it breathing. It doesn't move, as if nothing were going to happen. Because the room is old, the furniture creaks.

It's a bit frightening. The dead might awake. But that would only hurry the work with the knife. The sleeping figure raises the top fold of the sheet, turns over. But the sleeper goes on sleeping. It's a big body. Still, the bedclothes can be deceiving. Slowly, carefully, the intruder approaches, and stretches out a hand to touch the body gently. Sleeping, sleeping deeply, there's no reason the enemy should ever know a thing . . .

But that's no way to kill anyone. That's an assassin's way. And the intruder considers retracing his steps, making his way back along the route he came . . . No, it's not possible. Everything has been thoroughly thought out. It's only an instant, a short instant, and then . . .

It's impossible to turn back. The day will soon break, and in the daylight the man cannot, simply cannot stand the look in those eyes, the look that will stare into him, but without a shade of comprehension.

It will be necessary to take flight. To fly from the village, to go someplace where no one knows him, someplace where he can begin to hate again, with new hatreds. It takes years for a hatred to incubate. The man is no longer a child, and by the time a new hate grows and pounds in his pulse, his life will be done. His heart will no longer harbor bitterness and his arms, lifeless, and deprived of their strength, will fall by his side . . .

IT HAS BEEN almost a month since I've written anything at all. I've spent the time face down on the straw mattress, watching the hours go by, those hours which oftentimes seem to have wings, and then sometimes seem to be paralyzed. I've been letting my imagination soar, fly about freely, since it's the only thing about me that can soar or fly free. I've stared at the cracks and chips in the ceiling, trying to find likenesses to people I know. In this long month, in all truth, I've enjoyed life—in my own way—as I never had before, not in all the long years of my life, and that's a fact in spite of all my griefs and worries.

When peace descends on a sinner's soul it's like rain falling on fallow fields, slaking a desert's thirst, making the wasteland bloom. I say this because, although it took me much longer than it should have to find out that peace of soul is like a blessing from Heaven, the most precious benediction the poor and the confused can ever hope for, now that I know all this, now that loving peace and tranquility are my bedfellows, I enjoy it all with such a delight, almost a frenzy of delight, that I am much afraid lest I waste it in the short time left me—and the time left me is short enough indeed! It is quite probable that if such peace of soul had been within my reach some years back, by now I would have been a monk, a Carthusian at least, for this kind of inspired well-being would have persuaded me as much then as it does today. But God did not will it that way, and here I am locked up, with a sentence hanging over my head. Whether or not it would be better if the penalty were paid at once, or the agony prolonged, I don't know, but I must say I cling to these last days with more fervor—if that is the word—than I would cling to them had my life been an easy one. You will understand what I am trying to say.

During this long month spent in thought I knew every emotion: pain and pleasure, sadness and joy, faith and dissatisfaction and despair . . . God! What weak flesh you chose to test! I trembled as if I had a fever as one emotion gave way to another, and my eyes were flooded with fearful tears. Thirty days in a row are a long time to devote to thinking one and the same thought, to fostering the deepest guilt, and remorse, to be taken up solely with the idea that all one's past acts point straight to Hell . . . I envy the hermit whose holiness is written in his face, I envy the bird in his sky, his Heaven, the fish in his ocean, and I even envy the wild beast crouching in the undergrowth, for all of them are untroubled by memory. A past spent in sin is a heavy burden!

Yesterday I went to confession. I myself asked for the priest. The one who turned up was an ancient smooth-skinned man, Father Santiago Lurueña, good natured and yet distressed, kindly and as shriveled as an ant.

He is the chaplain, the one who says Sunday Mass for a hundred murderers, half a dozen guards, and two pairs of nuns.

I stood up when he came in.

"Good afternoon, Father."

"Greetings, my son. They tell me you sent for me."

"Yes, sir. I have."

He came up to me and kissed me on the forehead. It had been many years since anyone had kissed me.

"Is it to make confession?"

"Yes, Father, it is."

"You make me very happy, my son."

"I'm happy about it too, Father."

"God forgives us everything. He is very generous . . ."

"Yes, Father."

"And He is particularly happy to see strayed sheep return to the fold."

"Yes, Father."

"And to see the prodigal son return to his paternal home."

He held my hand tenderly in his, pressed against his cassock, and gazed into my eyes as if trying to make me understand.

"Faith is the light which guides our souls through the darkness of life."

"Yes."

"It's like a miraculous balm for wounded souls . . ."

Don Santiago was deeply moved. His voice trembled like that of a shy child. He smiled at me, and his smile was that of a saint.

"Do you know what confession is?"

I was ashamed to answer. But I had to admit, in the faintest of voices:

"Not very well."

"Don't worry, lad. Nobody is born knowing . . ."

Don Santiago explained some things I did not altogether understand. Doubtless he spoke the truth, for it sounded like the truth. We went on talking for a good while, almost the entire afternoon. When we stopped, the sun had already disappeared behind the horizon.

"Prepare yourself, Pascual, my son, to receive pardon, the pardon I give you in the name of our Lord God . . . Pray with me . . ."

When Don Santiago gave me his blessing, I had to make a great effort to receive it in all purity, without any sinister or vicious thoughts in my mind. I did my best, and received his blessing with the best intentions, I can assure you. I felt guilty and ashamed, terribly ashamed, but it was not at all as bad as I had expected it would be.

All last night I couldn't sleep a wink, and today I'm as tired and shaky as if I'd been flogged. However, since I've got the stack of paper I asked the warden to let me have, and since the only way to get out of the gloom is to cover all this paper with my scribbling, I'm going to try and begin again, to pick up the thread of the narrative and get this story on toward the end. It remains to be seen whether I'll have the necessary energy, for I'll need a good deal of it. Whenever I consider that if the schedules were to be speeded up at all, I'd find myself cut off in the middle of my account and would have to leave it in a sort of mutilated condition, whenever I think of that, I'm suddenly seized with an urge to write faster and faster. I must take hold of myself to keep from spurting ahead, for I know that writing as I do, with my five senses intent on the matter and proceeding ever so slowly, I still can't get the story said very clearly. And if I were to put it all down as it occurred to me, in one big rush, it would only be worse. The whole thing would get so out of hand and the account would be so garbled that its own father—me—would not recognize his offspring. Wherever memory plays a large part, as in this case, great care must be exercised because if things go wrong and events are placed in the wrong sequence, then there is no correction possible except to tear up all the papers written on and begin again. And I want to avoid such a course—a real danger— because seconds are never as good as firsts. Of course you may find all this concern of mine over minor matters most presumptuous, when all the major matters have gone so badly, and you may also think, and smile as you do, that it is very pretentious of me to avoid hurrying in order to give a good account of myself, when any educated person would carry it off quite naturally and with the greatest of ease, but if you will consider the effort represented by my having gone on writing for four months almost without letup, you will see that it is comparable to nothing else I have done in my lifetime, and you will perhaps find some excuse for my reasoning.

Things are never as they appear at first glance, and when we look closer, when we actually begin to work on something, we find strange and even unknown aspects, so that of our first impression sometimes not even the memory remains.

Such is the way with faces we imagine, with towns before we know them, which we picture in such and such a way, only to forget all our fancies at sight of the real thing. It is exactly the same with these papers of mine, these scribbled papers. At first I thought I would get them in order in a week. Today, after one hundred and twenty days, I have to smile just to think of my innocence.

I don't believe it can be a sin to recount crimes and outrages committed in the past if one has repented of them. Don Santiago himself told me to go ahead with my account, if it consoled me. And since it does, and since we must assume that Don Santiago knows what he is about when he speaks of these things, I don't expect God will be offended if I continue. Sometimes it hurts me to go over the ground, point by point, dwelling on the small and large details of my poor life. But then, by way of compensation, there are moments when the telling of my own story gives me the most honest of honest pleasures, perhaps because I feel so far removed from what I am telling that I seem to be repeating a story from hearsay about some unknown person. And what a difference there is between the actual past and the past as I would have it, if I were to begin again! But there's nothing to be done about all that, about all those things that can't be helped. A man has to stand up for what he's done, and see he doesn't repeat the worst of it, something I manage well enough, helped out in my stern purpose, it is true, by being locked up in here. I don't wish to overdo the note of meekness at this late hour in my life, for I can already hear you saying, "No fool like an old fool," which I'd rather you didn't say. And yet I'd like to put everything down just right, and assure you my life would have been exemplary had it run down the calm channel it does now.

I'll go on with my story. A month without writing is a long time for someone whose heartbeats are numbered, and too much tranquility for a man circumstances forced always to be restless.

I LOST NO time in preparing my flight. Some things allow no delay and this was one of them. I emptied the contents of my moneybox into my pocket, of the pantry into my saddlebag, and threw the ballast of my black thoughts and forebodings down the well. Like a thief in the night, I slipped away. Not exactly sure of where I was going, I set off along the high road, straight ahead and at such a fast pace that by dawn, as my aching bones told me, the village was a good three leagues behind me. Still I didn't want to slow down, inasmuch as I might even yet be recognized by someone in these parts. But I did snatch forty winks in an olive grove just off the road, and then had a bite from my supplies, and pushed on, intending to take the train as soon as I struck the railway line. People stared at me strangely, perhaps because I looked like a vagabond, and children trooped behind me in the villages, as they follow gypsies and halfwits. Far from annoying me, their inquisitive gaze and childish interest kept me company. If it had not been that I feared women—mothers—at that moment more than the plague, I would have gone so far as to make them a present of some little thing from my knapsack.

I caught the train in Don Benito, where I bought a ticket for Madrid. I was not intending to stay in the capital, but rather to go on to some city on the coast, and from there ship out to America. I had a good trip, for the coach I traveled in was nicely outfitted, and then, too, it was quite a novelty for me to watch the landscape go by as if it were lying on a sheet that some invisible hand was pulling. When everyone got off, I realized we were in Madrid. I was still so far away in my mind from the capital that my heart gave a leap, the same leap it always gives when face to face with reality, that any heart gives when something is almost on top of us, so close, and there's no turning back, when we had imagined it to be so far away.

I was well aware of the villainy and sharp practice in the big city, and it was after dark when we got there, just the time for the crooks and pickpockets to be operating at their best, and the likes of me easy game for them. So I decided that the best course of action would be to wait until daylight to look for lodgings. Meanwhile, I would have a bit of a nap on one of the numerous benches in the station. And that was what I did. I found one at the end of the hall, a little removed from the general bustle, and installed myself as comfortably as I could. With no more protection than my guardian angel over me, I fell as sound asleep as a stone, though I had intended to sleep the sleep of the partridge, one eye watching while the other one slept. And thus I slumbered until nearly daybreak. By the time I woke up, such cold had settled in my bones and such damp in my whole body, that I made up my mind it would be best if I didn't tarry there for another minute. I quit the station and, catching sight of a group of workers gathered around a street fire, I went up and joined them. They made me welcome and I was able to thaw my hide by standing in the heat of the blaze. At first the conversation was dull and dead, but then it picked up and came to life. Since they all seemed like good fellows, and as what I needed in Madrid was friends, I sent off an urchin who was hanging around to fetch a liter of wine for us all.

I never tasted a drop of that wine, and neither did my newfound pals, because the ragamuffin, who must have been sharper and more slippery than an eel, took the money and was never seen again. Since my idea had been to stand them all a swallow of wine, and though they laughed at the kid's trick, I still wanted to make friends with them. And so I waited until sunup, and then led them to a small café where I ordered glasses of coffee with milk all around, a move which served to win them over to me completely, each and every one of them was so grateful. I brought up the matter of lodgings, and one of them, whose name was Ángel Estévez, offered to put me up in his own house and to give me two meals a day, all for ten *reales*. The price didn't seem high to me then, for I didn't yet know that every day spent in his house in Madrid was to turn out to be twice as expensive at least, owing to the fact that Estévez would win the added sum off me nightly at a game called seven-and-a-half, of which both he and his wife were fanatical devotees.

I was not long in Madrid, not two weeks all told, and during that time I amused myself as cheaply as I could. I bought some little things I needed and which I picked up at a good price in the Calle de Postas and the Plaza Mayor. Every afternoon, about sundown, I would go and sit, for a peseta, in a singing café in the Calle de la Aduana. The "Edén Concert," it was called. And I would stay on there, watching the girls in the show, until near supper time, when I would make my way back to the Estévez garret in the Calle de la Ternera. He was usually there by the time I got in. His wife would bring out the stew, and we'd pitch in. Afterwards, we'd start up the card game, accompanied by two neighbors who came up every evening, sitting around the brazier table, our feet close to the glowing coals, and play until the early hours. I enjoyed that kind of life, and if it had not been that I was determined not to return to the village, I would have lingered in Madrid until my last céntimo was gone.

My host's house was like a dovecote, perched as it was on the roof, but since they never opened a window, even by way of doing anyone a favor, and inasmuch as the brazier was lit night and day, it wasn't bad sitting around the table with one's feet stretched under the thick folds of the tablecloth and one's toes to the coals. The room they'd given me had a ceiling which sloped down over the straw mattress in the corner, and more than once, until I got my bearings, I hit my head on a crossbeam which jutted out. Later, as I grew accustomed to the layout, I knew every nook and cranny and could have made my way to bed blindfolded. It's all a question of getting used to things.

Estévez's wife, whose name, as she told me herself, was Concepción Castillo López, was young, small, and she had a roguish little face that made her very appealing. And she was just as saucy and smart as Madrid women are supposed to be. She gave me the boldest looks, too, and spoke to me of anything she felt like without any hesitation at all. But she soon made it plain—just as soon as I put myself in a position for her to make it plain—that there was nothing doing as far as she was concerned, and that I needn't think there was. She was in love with her husband and he was the only man in the world for her. Too bad; it was a terrible shame, for she was a beauty and more pleasing than most, even though she was different from the women in my part of the country. But, since she never let me put my foot in at the door, and as I was a bit afraid of her anyway, she got farther and farther out of sight until the day came when I no longer gave her a thought as a woman. Her husband was as jealous as a sultan, and he must have had little faith in his wife, for he did not allow her to so much as peer down the stairwell. One Sunday afternoon, I remember, Estévez took it into his head to invite me to stroll through Retiro Park with himself and his wife, and he spent the entire afternoon calling her to order for casting glances at this man or that, or for obviously avoiding their glances. His wife took his accusations gracefully, even displaying a certain satisfaction, and with a look of loving tenderness on her face—which baffled me altogether, since it was so unlikely and unexpected. We walked up and down the path bordering the lake, and suddenly in the course of our stroll Estévez took to berating another stroller at the top of his voice. He shouted such a torrent of abuse at such speed, such outlandish phrases, that I could understand only half of what was going on. They were squabbling, apparently, because the other fellow had been looking Concepción over, appraising her. Still, I never have understood how, in view of the volley of insults they spat out, how they did not so much as raise their fists in a fighting pose, let alone actually come to blows. Their respective mothers were brought into it, they called each other great pimps and cuckolds at the top of their voices, they swore to eat each other's gizzards, but in the end they did not touch a hair of each other's heads, and that was the most curious thing of all. I was really agog at such goings-on, but as was only natural I did not interfere, though I was ready at any moment to rush to my friend's aid should he need me. When they got tired of dressing each other down they each went their separate ways, and nobody was any the worse for the experience.

What a pleasure! What fun! If we country men only had such gullets, and could swallow things the way city folk can, the prisons would be as empty as desert islands!

At the end of about two weeks, when I still did not know much about Madrid—not a city to be lightly skimmed—I decided to move on toward my eventual goal. I packed the small number of belongings I owned into a suitcase bought in the city, paid for a train ticket to the coast, and, accompanied by Estévez, who didn't let me out of his sight until the last moment, I made my way one day to the station—a different station than the one through which I'd entered the city. My destination was La Coruña, which I had been told was a port of departure for ships sailing to the Americas. The train trip to the sea was somewhat longer than my trip up to Madrid had been, for it was farther to go, but since there was a whole night to be passed in the course of it, and as I was not a man to be kept from sleep by motion or the noise of a train, it passed quicker than I had expected or than I had been led to expect by my fellow travelers. I had only been awake a few hours when I found myself beside the sea, and the sight of it was one of the most overwhelming things that ever happened to me, it seemed so enormous and vast.

As soon as I made my first arrangements in the port city I realized perfectly how simple-minded I had been in thinking that the few pesetas I had brought along in my pocket would be enough to get me to America. I had never until that moment known how expensive a sea voyage really is! I found my way to the steamship agency, made inquiries at one window, was sent to another, waited in a line that lasted no less than three hours, and then, when I moved up to speak to the employee, with the intention of discussing which course would be most convenient for me considering my finances, the man at the window, without a word turned halfway about and brought forth a paper which he shoved at me.

"Routes . . . fares . . . sailings from La Coruña on the fifth and twentieth of each month."

I tried to persuade him to talk to me, to discuss the matter of a voyage, but it was no use. He cut me off so short I was left in confusion.

"No use insisting."

I went off with my list of ports of call, price schedules, and the sailing dates fixed in my mind. What else could I do!

There was an artillery sergeant living in the house where
I took up lodgings, and he offered to decipher the papers
that had been handed me at the steamship agency. As soon
as he had figured out for me the price and the conditions of
payment, my soul fell into my feet, for I didn't have half the
amount necessary. The problem before me was no small one,
and I could imagine no solution. The artillery sergeant, whose
name was Adrián Nogueira, encouraged me to make the cross-
ing—he himself had been out there—and spoke glowingly of
Havana and even of New York. I must admit I listened to him
open-mouthed and felt more envious of him than I had ever
felt of anyone else before. It was obvious, however, that his
talk was only making my mouth water and nothing more, and
so one day I begged him to stop, for I had decided to stay and
not go over the seas. He pulled a face of rare bewilderment,
but being a man of discretion, as Galicians are known to be,
he did not mention the subject again.

My head was beginning to ache from so much thinking
about what I ought to do. Any solution but that of going back
to my village seemed acceptable, and so I took to doing whatever work was offered me. I carried luggage in the railroad
station and was a longshoreman on the docks, I worked in the
kitchen in the Hotel Ferrocarrilana, was night watchman for a
spell in the tobacco factory, and did a little bit of everything.
I wound up my port-city days living in La Apacha's place, in
the Calle del Papagayo,* on the left hand side of the street as
you ascend, where I made myself useful in a number of ways,
though my principal function was to bounce any customers
who had obviously come there only to raise hell.

I spent a year and a half at that house, which added up to a
total of nearly two years that I had been knocking about away
from home, and the accumulation of time made me think

---

* The place of the Lady Apache, on Parrot Street.

back—more than I would have expected—to what I had left behind. At first it was only at night, after I got into the bed they had set up for me in the kitchen, that I felt homesick, but then the hours of nostalgia began to increase, until the day arrived when the *morriña*, as they call it in La Coruña, the blues, began to seep into my soul, so that I could hardly wait to get back to my little home by the roadside. I was sure I'd be well received by my family—time heals everything— and the longing in me grew like mushrooms in the damp. It did not prove easy to borrow money, but with a little persistence—needed in any such matter—I finally got together what I needed. And so one fine day, after taking my leave of everyone who had befriended me, from La Apacha on down, I started out on the journey home, a journey bound to have a happy ending—had the Devil not done his worst in my house and made free with my wife while I was away, something I could hardly have known about at that moment. In all truth, it is only natural that my wife, still young and beautiful and with no guidance, should have gone astray for want of a husband and reacted to my running away, the worst sin I could have committed, the one I should never have committed, and one which God chose to punish me for, with a cruelty perhaps unnecessary . . .

A WEEK HAD passed since my return home, when my wife, who had received me, to all outward appearances at least, with the greatest affection and tenderness, woke me up to say:

"I've been thinking I was cold to you when you came back."

"Why, not at all!"

"I just wasn't expecting you, you know, I didn't expect to see you . . ."

"But now you're happy I've come back, aren't you?"

"Yes, now I'm glad . . ."

Lola seemed suddenly transfixed with sorrow. There was a great change in her.

"Did you think of me always? Did you remember me?" she asked.

"Always. Why do you think I've come back?"

My wife fell silent again.

"Two years is a long time . . ."

"A long time."

"And in the space of two years the world turns over quite a few times . . ."

"Only twice. A seaman in La Coruña told me so."

"Don't mention that place to me!"

"Why not?"

"Because I don't want it. I wish there was no such place as La Coruña!"

Her voice had a hollow ring. Her eyes were as dark as a forest at night.

"The world went around! Things change. There are always changes."

"Always."

"And in two years . . . I thought God must have carried you away."

"What are you trying to say?"

"Nothing!"

Lola began to cry bitterly. In a small voice she confessed:

"I'm going to have a baby."

"Another one?"

"Yes."

I felt a kind of fright.

"Whose is it?"

"Don't ask!"

"Don't ask? I want to know! I'm your husband!"

She let herself go. She burst out:

"My husband who wants to kill me! My husband who abandons me for two years! My husband who runs away from me as if I were a leper! My husband . . ."

"That's enough!"

Yes. It was better to stop there. My conscience told me that. It would be best to let time go by, to let the child be born . . . The neighbors would begin to talk about my wife's carryings-on. They'd begin to watch me out of the corners of their eyes, and to whisper as I went by . . .

"Do you want me to call Señora Engracia?"

"She's already seen me."

"What does she say?"

"That everything is going fine."

"It's not that . . . It's not that . . ."

"What is it, then?"

"Nothing . . . Only, it would be wise if we fixed everything up between ourselves."

My wife looked at me imploringly.

"Pascual, you wouldn't want to do that?"

"Yes, Lola, I would. And I wouldn't be the first man to think of it."

"Pascual, this child is stronger than the other, I feel he just has to live . . ."

"To shame and dishonor me!"

"Or to make you happy. How is anyone to know?"

"They'll know all right."

Lola smiled the smile of a child who has been hurt or mistreated. Her smile was painful to see.

"Maybe we can arrange things so that nobody will know."

"But they'll all know, I tell you."

I didn't want to be hard—God knows that—but the truth is that one is bound to convention like an ass to its halter.

If my position as a man would have allowed me to forgive, I would have forgiven her. But the world is the way it is, and to go against the current is useless.

"We'd better call her!"

"Who? Señora Engracia?"

"Yes."

"No, for God's sake, no! Am I to have another abortion? Always breeding just to breed? To bring forth dung?"

She threw herself on the floor to kiss my feet.

"I'll give you my life, all of it, if you want it!"

"I don't want it at all."

"My eyes and my blood, for having offended you!"

"That won't help either."

"My breasts, the hair of my head, my teeth! I'll give you whatever you want. Only just don't take away my child. It's the only reason for me to go on living!"

The best thing was to let her cry, cry as long as she wanted, until she was tired out, her nerves worn out, until she was finally quieted down, almost reasonable.

My mother, who must have been the bawd and go-between for everything that had happened, made herself scarce. She kept out of sight. The truth is pretty hot, and it burns a lot of people! She spoke to me as little as possible. She went out one door as I came in the other. She had my meals ready for me on time—something that never happened before and was not to happen again. It's sad to think that in order to gain a little peace a man has to make use of fear! She was so damned humble in her every move that she succeeded in unsettling me. I didn't care to discuss Lola's business with her.

That was something between the two of us, Lola and me, and it could only be settled between the two of us.

One day I called Lola to tell her:

"You don't need to worry any more."

"What do you mean?"

"No one is going to call Señora Engracia."

For one moment Lola was as still and thoughtful as a heron.

"You're very good to me, Pascual."

"Yes. At least, better than you think me."

"And better than I am."

"Let's not talk about that! Who was it?"

"Don't ask me that!"

"I'd rather know, Lola."

"But I'm afraid to tell you."

"You're afraid?"

"Yes, that you'll kill him."

"Does he mean so much to you, then?"

"He means nothing to me."

"In that case? . . ."

"It's just that blood seems a kind of fertilizer in your life . . ."

Her words stayed in my mind, as if they had been burned in, and just like a brand burned in me they will stay with me till I die.

"And if I were to swear to you that nothing would happen?"

"I wouldn't believe you."

"Why?"

"Because it just can't be, Pascual. You're too much of a man!"

"Thank God! But I still stand by my word."

Lola threw herself into my arms.

"I'd give years of my life if I could have spared us this!"

"I believe you."

"And to have you forgive me!"

"I forgive you, Lola. But you must tell me . . ."

"Yes."

She was paler than ever before, and her white face was contorted, so that I was suddenly fearful, horribly afraid that disaster had followed me home. I took her head in my hands, and caressed her. I spoke to her more tenderly than the most tender and faithful husband. I stroked her, against my shoulder, aware of everything she suffered, fearful she might faint if I asked the question again.

"Who was it?"

"Stretch!"

"Stretch?"

Lola did not answer.

She was dead. Her hair fell over her face, and her face fell down over her breasts . . . For a moment, she remained as she was, seated up against me, and then she suddenly fell away against the kitchen floor, against the worn cobbles of the floor . . .

A NEST OF vipers stirred in my chest. There was a scorpion in each drop of my blood, ready to sting. I set out to find the man who had killed my wife, ruined my sister, and made my life as bitter as it was. It wasn't easy to find him, for he took to his heels. He heard I was after him, and he put a good distance between us. He was not seen around Almendralejo for four months. I dropped into Nieves' place, and saw Rosario . . . What a change I found in her! She had aged, her face was prematurely wrinkled, there were black shadows under her eyes, and her hair hung lank. It was painful to look at her, and remember how good looking she had been.

"What have you come for?"

"I've come looking for a man!"

"It wouldn't be much of a man who runs from his enemy."

"Not much . . ."

"Not much of a man who wouldn't be waiting for a visit that was expected."

"Not much . . . Where is he?"

"I don't know. He went away yesterday."

"Where did he go?"

"I don't know."

"Don't you?"

"No."

"Are you sure?"

"As sure as the sun is shining."

She seemed to be telling the truth. She was soon enough

to prove her affection, when she came home to look after me, quitting that house and Stretch with it.

"Do you know if he's far off?"

"He didn't tell me anything."

There was nothing for it but to bury my anger. To vent the wrath one feels for a blackguard upon some innocent creature has never been the man's way.

"Did you know what was going on?"

"Yes."

"And you kept it so quiet?"

"Who was I to tell?"

"No, of course, nobody."

True enough, there was nobody for her to tell. There are things which are not of equal interest to everyone, things which we must bear on our own backs alone, like a martyr's cross, and keep to ourselves. We can't tell people everything that's going on inside us. In most cases they wouldn't even know what we were talking about.

Rosario came away with me.

"I don't want to stay here another day. I'm beat."

And so she came home. She seemed almost frightened. And she was devoted and more hard-working than I had ever seen her. She took care of me with a gentleness I could not— and now, what is worse, never can—repay, or even sufficiently show my gratitude for. There was always a clean shirt ready for me. She saw to it that my money went as far as possible. She kept my meals hot, if I was late in getting home . . . It was a pleasure to live like that! The days went by as smoothly as feathers downwind. The nights were as peaceful as nights in a convent. And the black thoughts which had plagued me seemed to vanish. How far away were the troubled times in La Coruña! And the knife-fighting days! They seemed, almost, to have gotten lost in my memory. Even the wound left by Lola was beginning to heal. The past was becoming dim, when suddenly my unlucky star, that evil star which seemed bent on destroying me, brought it all back, for my undoing.

It was in Martinete's tavern. Señorito Sebastián spoke up:

"Have you seen Stretch?"

"No. Why?"

"No reason. Only, they say he's been seen around."

"In the village?"

"That's what they say."

"You wouldn't be making a fool of me, now?"

"Don't get worked up. I tell it to you just as it was told to me. Why would I want to make a fool of you, now?"

I couldn't wait to find out what truth there was in his words. I ran all the way home. I streaked along like a flash of lightning, unmindful of the ups and downs of the terrain. I found my mother standing in the doorway.

"Where's Rosario?"

"She's inside."

"Alone?"

"Yes, why?"

I didn't answer. I went on back into the kitchen, and found her there, stirring something on the stove.

"Have you seen him? Stretch?"

Rosario gave a start. She raised her head slowly. She was calm, or appeared so outwardly, when she answered:

"Why do you ask me?"

"Because he's been seen in the village."

"In the village?"

"That's what I've been told."

"Well he hasn't been around here."

"Are you sure?"

"I swear it."

She didn't have to swear it to me. It was true enough. He

hadn't gotten there yet, though he would shortly, as bold as brass and proud as a peacock, a regular gypsy from the south.

He found my mother guarding the door.

"Pascual here?"

"What do you want with him?"

"Nothing at all. Just a little business matter."

"What business?"

"A little business we have between us."

"Go on in. You'll find him in the kitchen."

He came on in without taking off his cap. He walked in whistling a tune.

"*Hola*, Pascual!"

"*Hola*, Paco! Take your cap off. You're indoors."

He took off his cap.

"If that's what you want!"

He was acting the cool one, the man in control of himself. But he wasn't quite successful. It was obvious he was a bit nervous, perhaps scared.

"*Hola*, Rosario!"

"*Hola*, Paco!"

My sister smiled a cowardly smile. It made me sick. He smiled at her, too, but his lips seemed to have been drained of all their color.

"Do you know why I'm here?"

"You tell us."

"To fetch Rosario!"

"That's what I thought. Stretch, you're not taking Rosario anywhere."

"I'm not?"

"No."

"Who's going to stop me?"

"Me."

"You?"

"Yes, me. Or do you think I'm not enough?"

"You're not much . . ."

I was as cold-blooded as a lizard, at that moment. I knew well enough what I was about and how far I would have to go. I squared away, calculated the distance between us and, allowing for no further talk—so that what happened the time before should not happen again—I swung a stool right into the middle of his face. He was hit so hard that he went over backwards and lay like a dead man up against the fireplace. A moment later he struggled to get up, drawing his knife the while. His face was full of malice, a fright to see. But his shoulder bones had been crushed, and he couldn't really move. I grabbed hold of him and dragged him to the edge of the road, and there I pushed him down.

"Stretch, you killed my wife . . ."

"Your wife was a whore!"

"Whatever she was, you killed her. And you dishonored my sister . . ."

"She was good and dishonored when I took her up!"

"She might have been, but you finished her off! It's time for you to shut your mouth, anyway. You dogged my steps and now you've found me. I didn't want to hurt you, or break your damned bones . . ."

"They'll mend soon enough, and when they do . . . !"

"What then?"

"I'll shoot you down like a mad dog!"

"Remember that I've got you where I want you right now!"

"You wouldn't know how to kill me!"

"I wouldn't?"

"No."

"What makes you think that? You're pretty sure of yourself!"

"Because the man who can kill me hasn't been born yet!"

He was brave enough.

"You want to get on now?"

"I'll go when I feel like it!"

"Which is right now!"

"Give me Rosario!"

"I won't!"

"Give her to me, or I'll kill you!"

"A little less talk about killing. You're in a bad enough way as it is."

Stretch made a supreme effort. He lurched to his feet and tried to push past me toward Rosario.

I took him by the throat and forced him back onto the ground.

"Out of my way!"

"Not on your life!"

We grappled. I flattened him against the earth. With one knee on his chest I told him the truth. I confessed it to him:

"I'm not killing you because I promised her I wouldn't . . ."

"Who'd you promise?"

"Lola."

"So, she still loved me?"

That was going too far. It was too much for me to take. My hands tightened. I pushed a bit harder . . . The flesh of his chest made the same sound as a piece of meat turning on a spit . . . Blood began to pour from his mouth. When I stood up, his head fell sideways, very gently . . .

I WAS KEPT locked up for three years, three long years, as long as the street of sorrow. At first it seemed my sentence would never end. Long afterwards, the years seemed like a dream. Three years working, day after day, in the prison shoemaker's shop. I was very happy to get a few minutes of sun in the yard during rest periods. I watched the hours passing, watched them with anxiety, and then, because of good conduct, my original sentence was reduced—to my undoing—before it was fully served.

There's matter for thought in the fact that on the few occasions in my life when I decided not to act too badly, my evil fate, the evil star I mentioned before, took special pleasure in dogging me. It blighted everything so thoroughly that not a single good deed was of any use whatsoever. Worse than that: not only was anything that might be called good of no earthly use to me, but it was always so warped and twisted that in the end it only made matters worse. If I had acted up, if I could have shown bad conduct, I would have stayed in the Chinchilla Prison the full twenty-eight years of my sentence. I would have stayed there, and rotted alive, like the other prisoners. I would have been madly bored, no doubt, have despaired, would have cursed enough, but there I'd still be, expiating past crimes, but free of new ones, a captive and a prisoner—no question of that—but with my head as secure on my shoulders as the day I was born, free of guilt, unless it was the guilt which comes from original sin. If I had acted

neither one way nor the other, demonstrated neither good
conduct nor bad, like almost everyone else, my twenty-eight
years would have come out to about fourteen or fifteen, and
my mother would have died a natural death by the time I got
out, my sister Rosario would have lost her youth, and with her
youth her beauty, and with her beauty the danger to which she
was exposed, and I—this wretch, this example of a defeated
man, who can arouse so little compassion in you or in society—would have emerged as mild as a lamb, as soft as a woolly
blanket, far from the danger of a new fall. At this very moment
I might well be living in peace somewhere or other, engaged
in some sort of gainful work, enough to earn my keep, trying
to forget the past and looking toward the future. I might even
have succeeded in my efforts . . . But instead I distinguished
myself by my good conduct in prison, put on the best face I
could in poor circumstances, exceeded myself in carrying out
the orders given me, managed to soften the carrying-out of
the law, and earned good reports from the warden . . . And so
they let me out. They opened the gates, and turned me out,
without defenses, into the very midst of Evil. They told me:

"You've served your sentence, Pascual. Back to the struggle, back to life, back to putting up with everybody else, to
dealing with everyone, to rubbing shoulders and bumping up
against them . . ."

And, thinking they were doing me a favor, they sank me
for good.

This philosophy of mine did not come to me the first
time I wrote this section and the following two chapters. But
the first draft of this part of the story was stolen from me—
though I still can't understand why. The theft may strike you
as so unlikely that you will not believe what I am saying. But
nevertheless, I was much saddened by this meaningless theft
and exhausted by the work of repeating what I had already

written. My memory was forced and my ideas magnified out of all proportion, and thus was born my philosophizing. I don't think my penitence—which is as great as my poorness of spirit will allow, though it may be too small to cover my sins—would in any way be served by my suppressing my own words, and therefore I incorporate these wordy thoughts in my story, just as they occur to me, and I leave you to judge them as you think best.

When I came out of prison, I found the countryside gloomier, far gloomier than I had expected. As I pictured it to myself in prison, I had imagined it—don't ask me why—all green and lovely meadows, speckled with bursting wheatfields, peopled with farmers happily at work from dawn to dusk, their heads free from every evil thought and their wineskins not far off. And there it was, parched and sterile, worse than a cemetery, as empty of human presence as a local country shrine the day after the feast-day pilgrimage of the patron saint . . .

Chinchilla is a bleak and gloomy spot, like all the villages in La Mancha, defeated and crushed as if by some great sorrow, gray and grim, the same as any place where the natives never poke their heads out of doors. I didn't stay around there any longer than was necessary before catching the train which would take me back to my own, to my house and my family; back to the town I was sure to find in the same place, my house that would be shining in the sun like a jewel, my family who thought me far away and would not be expecting that I would soon be among them: my mother whom God might have made more tender in these three long years, and my sister, my dear sister, my blessed sister who would jump with joy at the sight of me.

The train took a long time, a very long time, in getting in to the Chinchilla station. It was strange that a man who had waited so many hours, who had so many hours of waiting worked into his body and soul, should have shown such impatience over another hour more or less. But the fact is that such was the case: I was impatient, I fretted, I was undone, as if some great enterprise were at hand and couldn't wait. I strode up and down the station, went over to the canteen, walked around a neighboring field . . . There was nothing for it. The train didn't come, it wouldn't come, there was no sign of it yet. For all its being late, it seemed farther away than ever. I thought of the prison, still visible in the near distance, over behind the station. It seemed empty, deserted, but I knew it was filled to the walls with a heap of unfortunate wretches, whose lives could have taken up as many hundreds of pages as there were prisoners. I thought of the warden, of the last time I saw him. He was a little bald old man, with a white mustache and eyes as blue as the sky. His name was Don Conrado. I had come to love him as a father, and was grateful to him for the kind words of comfort he had found occasion to address me. The last time I had seen him was in his office, where he had summoned me.

"By your leave, Don Conrado."

"Do come in, son."

His voice was already weak with age and failing health, and, when he called any of us "son," it seemed to grow even more tender and to tremble as it passed through his lips. He had me sit across the table from him, held out his great tobacco pouch made of goatskin, and produced a little packet of cigarette paper, which he offered me, too.

"Cigarette?"

"Thank you, Don Conrado."

Don Conrado laughed.

"Talking to you, it's best to do it through a cloud of smoke. That way one sees less of that ugly mug of yours!"

He ended his remark with a great guffaw, which, at the end turned into a coughing fit. It went on until he almost choked and it left him wheezing and red as a tomato. He grabbed the handle of a drawer, pulled it open, and brought out a bottle of brandy and two glasses. I was startled: he had always treated me well, that was true enough, but never that well.

"What's the matter, Don Conrado?"

"Nothing, my boy, nothing at all . . . Come on, now, have a drink . . . To your freedom!"

He was convulsed again by his cough. I was about to ask: "To my liberty?"

But he waved his hand at me to keep quiet. This time it was the other way around: what had begun as a cough ended in a guffaw.

"Yes. The worst rascals have the best luck!"

And he went on laughing, happy to be able to tell me the news, glad to be throwing me out into the street. Poor Don Conrado! Such a good man! If only he had known that the best thing that could have happened to me was to be kept right there! When I did come back to Chinchilla, to that house, he told me as much, with tears in his eyes, in those eyes only slightly more blue than his tears.

"Well now, let's be serious. Read this . . ."

He showed me the order for my release. I couldn't believe my eyes.

"Have you read it?" he asked a moment later.

"Yes, sir."

He opened a folder and took out two papers, duplicates. It was the order for my discharge.

"This one is for you. You can go anywhere with this paper. Sign here, without making a mess."

I folded the paper and stuck it in my wallet . . . I was a free man! I would never be able to explain what went on inside me at that moment. Don Conrado became serious. And then he delivered a lecture on honesty and good habits. He gave me some advice on not giving way to impulses: if I had kept his words in mind I would have saved myself more than one sad wrangle. When he was through, he handed me, as a kind of final flourish, twenty-five pesetas in the name of the Ladies' Society for the Rehabilitation of Prisoners, a charitable institution with headquarters in Madrid and dedicated to aiding us.

He pressed a button, a bell sounded, and a prison official appeared. Don Conrado stretched out his hand to me.

"Goodbye, son. May God watch over you!"

I could scarcely contain my sudden joy. Don Conrado turned to the official.

"Muñoz, accompany this gentleman as far as the gate. First take him to the Administration building, though, for he has a week's allowance due him."

I was never to see Muñoz again in this life, but I did see Don Conrado—three and a half years later.

At last the train arrived. Sooner or later, everything comes in this life, except forgiveness from those one has wronged, and that seems to hold off perversely. I found a seat in a compartment, and then, after being jolted about for a day and a half, we reached the village, whose station was still fresh in my mind, so to say, for I had been thinking about it all through that voyage. Nobody, absolutely nobody, unless it were God on high, knew that I was coming, and nevertheless—I don't know what kind of mania possessed me—for one fleeting moment I was under the distinct impression the platform would be swarming with joyful people who would receive me with their open arms held high, waving handkerchiefs and shouting my name to the four winds.

When I stepped off the train, an icy pang as sharp as a dagger stabbed me to the heart. There was no one in the

station. It was night. The stationmaster, Señor Gregorio, with
the lantern which was green on one side and red on the other
and his signal flag already rolled up in its tin case, had just
signaled the train to move on.

Now he would turn around and see me, recognize me and
congratulate me.

"*Caramba*, Pascual! You back here?"

"Yes, Señor Gregorio. A free man!"

"Well, I'll be damned!"

And without further ado, he turned on his heel and strode
into his hut. I wanted to shout after him:

"I'm free, Senor Gregorio! I'm a free man!" For I thought
he must not have understood. But I hesitated, and then I
didn't call.

The blood throbbed in my head and the tears almost
welled up into my eyes. Señor Gregorio wasn't interested in
my liberty, he didn't give a damn whether I was free or not.

I went out of the station carrying all my belongings in the
bundle over my shoulder and set off down a footpath that
bypassed the town and would take me to the main road where
my house stood. I was downcast, sad as could be. All my joy
had been blasted by Señor Gregorio and his coldness. A torrent of gloomy thoughts, of dire presentiments flooded my
mind, and I strove in vain to keep them back. It was a clear
night, without a single cloud, and the moon stood fixed in the
sky, like the Sacred Host held aloft. I tried to avoid thinking
of the terrible cold seeping through me.

A little further on, to the right of my road and halfway
home, the cemetery lay along my way, just where it had always
lain, and bounded by the same wall of blackened adobe bricks,
with the same tall cypress which hadn't changed a leaf and the
same hooting owl perched in its branches. It was the cemetery
where my father rested from his ruinous fury, Mario from his

innocence, my wife from her abandon, and Stretch from his pimping. It was the cemetery where the remains of my two children lay rotting, the one who had been aborted, and yet buried, and Pascualillo who in the eleven months of his life had yet been our darling . . .

I hated to arrive home this way, alone, in the night, greeted first by my dead in the village cemetery! It seemed as if Providence had made me come this way, as if it took delight in putting the cemetery in my way, so that I might be plunged into the depths, thinking on how all of us are nothing!

My shadow jogged on before me, a long ghostly shadow, stretched out across the earth, following its contours, first straight down the road and then up the cemetery wall as if anxious to peer inside. I broke into a run, and my shadow ran too. I stopped, and so did my shadow. I gazed around the firmament: there was not a cloud to be seen in its great semicircle. My shadow would be sure to accompany me, step by step, until I got home.

I was seized with fright, an inexplicable fright. I imagined I saw the dead, in the form of skeletons, coming out of their tombs to watch me passing by. I didn't dare raise my eyes. And I quickened my pace. My body seemed to have lost its weight, and so did my bundle. And yet I seemed to have grown stronger. Suddenly, I was running like a scared hound. Then I galloped like a runaway horse. I ran and ran. I was like a madman, like someone possessed. By the time I reached my house I was exhausted. I couldn't have taken another step . . .

I put down my bundle, and sat on top of it. There was not a sound to be heard. Rosario and my mother were sure to be sleeping soundly, all unaware that I had arrived, that I was free, only a few steps away. Perhaps my sister had said a Salve Regina—her favorite prayer—for my release, just before getting into bed! Perhaps at that very moment she was dreaming sadly of my misfortune, imagining me stretched on the wood floor of my cell dreaming of her as she dreamt of me, for she knew that my affection for her was the one true feeling I had ever felt in my life! She might even be in a panic, laboring in the toils of a nightmare!

And there I was, sound as an apple, back from prison and ready to begin all over again, ready to console her, to take care of her, to see her smile.

I didn't know what to do. I could knock at the door, call out to them . . . But that would only scare them, upset them at best. No one comes calling at such an hour. They might not even open the door. Still, I couldn't go on sitting there on my bundle, waiting for daylight.

Just then two men came walking up the road. They were talking in loud voices, and were in a carefree mood, quite oblivious and happy. They were coming from the direction of Almendralejo; perhaps they had been seeing their girlfriends. I soon recognized them: León, who was Martinete the innkeeper's brother, and Señorito Sebastián. I hid. I don't know why, but the sight of them made me scurry.

They passed quite close to the house, quite close to me, and I could clearly hear what they said.

"Well, look what happened to Pascual, now."

"And he hadn't done any more than any one of us would have done."

"Defended his wife's honor."

"Exactly."

"And there he is in Chinchilla, more than a day's train ride away, going on three years now . . ."

I was deeply moved, moved to joy. The idea of coming out of hiding, of presenting myself before them, of embracing them in greeting flashed through my mind . . . But I decided against it. In prison I had learned to be calm, to check my impulses.

I waited for them to pass on. When I was sure they were far enough away, I emerged from the ditch where I had been hiding, and went up to the door. My bundle was still there, they hadn't even seen it. If they had seen it, they would have approached, and then I would have had to come out and explain. They would have been convinced I was in hiding, in flight.

I didn't want to think about it any more. I knocked at the door twice. No one answered. I waited a few moments. Nothing happened. I knocked again, harder this time. Inside, someone lit a candle.

"Who is it?"

"It's me!"

"Who?"

It was the voice of my mother. I was happy to hear her—why deny it?

"Me, Pascual."

"Pascual?"

"Yes, Mother, Pascual!"

She opened the door. In the light of the candle she looked like a witch.

"What do you want?"

"What do I want?"

"Yes."

"I want to go in. What would I want?"

She was certainly acting odd. Why should she treat me like that?

"What's the matter with you, Mother?"

"Nothing—why?"

"You seem kind of . . . stony."

I would have sworn my mother would rather not have seen me back. All my past hatred welled up in me. I tried to master myself.

"And Rosario?"

"She's gone."

"Gone?"

"Yes."

"Where?"

"To Almendralejo."

"Again?"

"Again"

"Is she with someone?"

"Yes."

"Who?"

"What do you care?"

The world seemed to fall apart. I couldn't see. I wondered if I wasn't dreaming. For a moment neither of us spoke.

"Why did she go away?"

"That's the way things are!"

"Couldn't she have waited for me?"

"She didn't know you were coming. But she did always talk about you . . ."

"Did you go hungry?"

"Sometimes."

"Is that why she left?"

"Who knows?"

We fell silent again.

"Do you ever see her?"

"Yes. She comes home often. Especially since he lives here too."

"He?"

"Yes."

"Who is it?"

"Señorito Sebastián."

I thought I would drop dead. I would have paid money to have been back in prison.

ROSARIO CAME TO see me as soon as she found out I was back.

"I heard yesterday you were home. You can't imagine how happy I was to hear it!"

And how happy I was to hear her say so!

"I know it, Rosario, I can imagine it. Because I was just as anxious to see you!"

We seemed to be making formal remarks, polite flattery, as if we had only just met, ten minutes before. We were both trying hard to sound natural.

"How did you come to go away again?"

"You know how it is . . ."

"Were you so badly off?"

"Bad enough."

"And you couldn't wait?"

"I didn't want to."

Her voice grew harsh.

"I didn't feel like going through any more disasters . . ."

I understood. It was clear. The poor girl had already stood enough.

"Let's not talk about it, Pascual."

Rosario smiled the way she always smiled, a sad and rather weary smile, the kind of smile you see on the faces of all unfortunates who are good-hearted.

"Let's talk about something else . . . Do you know that I've found a girl for you?"

"For me?"

"Yes."

"A girl?"

"Yes, of course. Why does it seem so strange?"

"No, it doesn't, but it does sound odd. Who could there be that would like me?"

"Any woman. Or do you think I don't love you, either?"

I liked hearing my sister say she cared for me, even though I already knew how she felt. And I liked her wanting to find a girl for me, too. What a fine idea!

"And who is she?"

"Señora Engracia's niece."

"Esperanza?"

"Yes."

"A fine-looking girl!"

"Who has been in love with you since before you got married."

"She was pretty quiet about it!"

"What do you expect? Everyone is the way they are."

"And what have you told her?"

"Nothing . . . Only that one day you would come back."

"And I've come back . . ."

"Thank God!"

The girl Rosario had picked for me really was a stunning woman. She was not exactly Lola's type, in fact quite different, something like halfway between her and the wife of Estévez, and if you looked closely, somewhat similar in build to my sister. She was probably just past thirty, only she didn't seem that old, she was so well preserved and youthful in appearance. She was very religious, and even vaguely mystical, something rare enough in those parts. She let herself be carried along by life, like the gypsies do, her belief fixed in the words she used to repeat:

"Why change? Why try to change? It is written!"

She lived up the hill with her aunt, Señora Engracia, who was a stepsister to the girl's long-dead father. Esperanza had in fact been left a total orphan while still very young. She was by nature agreeable and rather shy, and no one could say he had ever seen or heard her arguing or quarreling, least of all with her aunt, whom she held in the greatest respect. She was more cleanly than most women, had the color of apples in her cheeks, and when, a short time later, she became my wife—my second wife—she put my house in such order that nobody would ever have recognized the place.

The first time, though, that we met face to face after my return, it was pretty embarrassing for us both. We both knew what we had to say to each other, and we both watched each other with shy slyness, like two spies, trying to catch some sign . . .

We were left alone, but that didn't help matters. After we had been together for a whole hour, it seemed as if each time we tried to start up the conversation it became all the harder. It was she who finally broke the ice:

"You're much stouter."

"Maybe . . ."

"And you're looking stronger."

"That's what they tell me . . ."

I was making inward efforts to appear affable and yet decisive, but I was getting nowhere. To all appearances I was a dummy, and I felt overwhelmed, suffocated, and yet—in all my life I can never remember a more pleasant feeling, and one that I more regret losing.

"What's it like there?"

"No good."

She grew pensive. Who knows what was going on in her mind!

"Did you think of Lola very often?"

"Sometimes. Why deny it? Since I had the whole day to think in, I thought about everyone. Even Stretch!"

Esperanza seemed even paler.

"I'm very happy you've come back."

"Yes, Esperanza, and I'm very glad you waited for me."

"Waited for you?"

"Yes. Didn't you?"

"Who told you?"

"Oh, everything gets around! There aren't any secrets."

Her voice trembled, and I was on the point of catching her tremor and letting it affect my voice.

"Was it Rosario?"

"Yes. Is there anything wrong in that?"

"Nothing."

The tears came to her eyes.

"What must you have thought of me?"

"What would you have me think? That's not wrong, either."

I came to her slowly and kissed her hands. She let me kiss them.

"I'm as free as you, Esperanza."

* * *

"As free as when I was twenty."

Esperanza looked at me timidly.

"I'm not very old now. And I have to think of going on living."

"Yes."

"To think about my work, my house, my life . . . Were you really waiting for me?"

"Yes."

"Then why not say so?"

"I've already told you."

That was true. She had already let me know, but I took pleasure in having her tell me again.

"Tell me again."

Esperanza was blushing as red as a pepper. Her voice was short-breathed, faint, and her lips and nostrils trembled like leaves in the wind, like the plumage of a linnet basking and fluffing in the sun.

"I waited for you, Pascual. Every day I said a prayer for you to come back soon. God listened to me."

"That's true."

I kissed her hands again. Inside me I felt weak, almost faint. I didn't dare kiss her face.

"Would you . . . ? Would you . . . ?"

"Yes."

"Do you know what I was trying to say?"

"Yes. You don't have to say it."

Suddenly she was as radiant as a sunrise.

"Pascual, kiss me . . ."

Her voice was lower, secretive, husky, almost shameless.

"I waited for you long enough!"

I kissed her passionately, deeply, and yet with an adoration I had never felt toward any woman, and I clung to her for so long a time, that when I released her at last a most faithful tenderness had been born within me.

WE HAD BEEN married about two months when I began to realize that my mother was making use of the same evil arts, the same tricks she had used before I had been sent to the penitentiary. It made my blood boil to see her always sullen, wearing a surly, almost scornful expression, to hear her deliberately pointed and cutting remarks, the tone of voice she always used with me, a kind of mocking falsetto, as false as the rest of her. She could not get along with my wife, though she tolerated her in the house, since there was nothing she could do about that. She concealed her dislike so poorly that Esperanza, one day when she had stood about as much as she could, made it clear to me that the only solution we would ever find would be to put ground between ourselves and her. This country expression "put ground between" is used when two people arrange to live in villages at some distance from each other, but strictly speaking, it could also refer to the ground on which one person walks and in which another sleeps, a distance in depth of only a few feet.

I turned over and over in my mind the idea of moving away. I thought of going to La Coruña, or to Madrid, or closer by, toward the provincial capital at Badajoz. But the fact remained, I don't know whether due to my cowardice or my lack of decision, that I kept putting it off, and putting it off.

By the time I did run away, it was with the burning need to "put ground between" me and my own flesh, to put the earth between me and my memory, between me—and no one else.

And the earth was not wide enough to put between me and my crime. It was not long enough or deep enough to deaden the clamor of my own conscience.

I wanted to put ground between my shadow and myself, between my name and me, between the memory of my name and the rest of me, between my flesh and me myself, that me myself who, without shadow and name and memory and flesh would be almost nothing.

There are times when the best course is to sink out of sight like the dead, disappear in one fell swoop as if swallowed up by the earth, to vanish into thin air like a puff of smoke. But it is never quite possible to do any of these things. If it were, we would be transformed into angels, for we would thus be able at will to extricate ourselves from the mud of crime and sin, we would be freed from the weight of our tainted flesh, a dead weight which we would never miss or long for again—such honor it would come to hold for us. But there is always someone who won't let us forget our flesh, someone to rub our noses, our souls' noses, in the dregs. And nothing reeks like the leprous stench left in us by past evil, or like the hopeless rot choking us in that charnel-house of aborted hopes which is all our sad life amounts to almost from birth!

The idea of death comes upon us with the slow gait of a wolf or the tarrying glide of a serpent, like any and all of our dread imaginings, like all dreadful ideas which hurl us to the ground. Sudden starts suffocate us for a moment, but then they are gone, and we go on living. The thoughts that drive us to the worst forms of madness, to the deep brooding of sadness, always approach stealthily and slowly and almost unperceived, just as the fog invades the fields or consumption the lungs. They come on slowly, unhurried, as regular as the beat of a pulse—but fatally, implacably. Today we notice nothing. Perhaps tomorrow we notice nothing either, nor the day after tomorrow, nor nothing for a whole month through. But then the month is done, and our food turns bitter, and all remembrance is painful. We are touched, smitten and doomed. As the days and nights succeed each other we begin to grow solitary, withdrawn. Our minds begin to seethe with ideas, ideas which lead to our losing our heads on the chopping-block, where they are cut off perhaps merely to prevent their continuing to seethe so atrociously.

We may spend weeks in the same condition, without any change. The people around us become accustomed to our sullen gloom, our strange behavior no longer strikes them as strange. But then one day the evil grows, like a young tree, and fattens, and now we no longer speak to anyone. Once again we become an object of curiosity, as if we were a lover mooning with love. We get thinner and thinner, and our once bristly beard grows lanker each day. We begin to droop from the hatred consuming us. We can no longer stand to look into another person's eyes. Our conscience burns in us: but, so much the better, let it burn! Our eyes smart, they brim with poison whenever we take a good look around. The enemy is aware of our anguish, but he is confident: instinct doesn't lie. Disaster seems joyful, beckoning, and we take the most tender pleasure in dragging it across the immense plaza of broken glass which our soul has become. When we begin to bolt like a fallow deer, when we start up from dreams, we are altogether undermined by the evil. There is no longer any solution left, no escape, no compromise. We begin to fall, precipitously, and never again will raise our heads in this life. Unless it be for one final look, to watch our own headlong fall into Hell.

My mother took a constant delight in exciting my anger and my manias, which were multiplying like flies around a corpse. The gall I swallowed was choking my heart. My thoughts became so black that I grew frightened at my own anger. I could no longer look at her. The days were all alike now, the same pain gnawing at my entrails, the same forebodings clouding my vision.

The day I decided I would have to use my knife on her, I was so weary of it all, so convinced in my bones that bloodletting was the only cure, that the thought of her dying didn't even quicken my pulse. It was something fated, it had to be and would be. It was something I would bring about and could not avoid bringing about even if I wanted. It was impossible for me to change my mind, turn back, avoid what I would right now give an arm to have avoided doing, but which at that time I carefully and delightedly planned with the calculation and premeditation a farmer devotes to his fields of wheat.

Everything was in readiness. I spent whole nights going over the selfsame ground so as to screw my courage to the sticking point and marshal all my strength. I sharpened my hunting knife: its long broad blade was like the leaf on a cornstalk, its mother-of-pearl handle lent it a provocative air, and it sported a little groove running its width. All that was left was to decide on a date. And then, no faltering, no turning back, but an end to the job whatever the cost, and always, the need to keep my wits about me. I must strike home, a clean blow, and then get away, far away, to La Coruña, or someplace where nobody could possibly know about what happened, and where I would be allowed to live in peace while waiting for everyone to forget, for the oblivion that would allow me to return and start life anew.

My conscience did not trouble me. There was no reason why it should. Consciences bite and prick only when an injustice has been committed, such as drubbing a child or potting a swallow on the wing. But when hate leads us by the hand, when we are in the throes of an obsession which numbs and overwhelms us, we need never feel the pangs of repentance, and our conscience need never bite and prick us.

It was on the tenth of February of 1922. That year the tenth of February fell on a Friday. It was a clear day, as was only fitting in that part of the country at that time. The sun felt grand, and I seem to remember that there were more children than ever in the plaza, playing jacks and marbles. This circumstance gave me pause. But I got the better of myself. It would have been unthinkable to have turned back, it would have been fatal, it would have led to my death, perhaps to suicide. I'd have ended up at the bottom of the Guadiana, or under the wheels of a train . . . No, it was impossible to retreat, the only way was forward, always forward, until the end. It had become a matter of personal pride.

My wife must have noticed something strange about me.

"What are you planning to do?"

"Nothing. Why?"

"I don't know. You act so odd."

"You're imagining things!"

I kissed her, to ease her spirit. It was the last kiss I ever gave her. How far I was from knowing that! If I had known, I might have shuddered.

"What's the kiss for?"

Her question brought me up short.

"Why shouldn't I give you a kiss?"

I thought over her words. She seemed to know all about what was going to happen, as if she had already walked down that particular street.

The sun set in the same place it did every day. Night came. We ate our supper. The women got into bed. I stayed behind, as usual, to poke around in the ashes in the fireplace. I had long since given up going to Martinete's tavern.

The time had come. I had waited long enough. I must pluck up courage, and get it done, and done as quickly as possible. The night is short, and everything must be finished in the dark. By dawn I must be far from the village, many leagues away.

For a long time I just listened. Nothing could be heard. I went to my wife's room. She was sleeping. I let her sleep. My mother, too, would surely be asleep. I went back into the kitchen and took off my shoes. The floor was cold, and the stones of the paving were hard against the bottom of my feet. I took my knife out of its sheath. It flashed in the firelight like the rays of the sun.

There she lay, under the sheets, her face pressed into the pillow. I had only to hurl myself on that body and drive the knife home. She wouldn't move, or let out a cry. She wouldn't have time . . . There she was at last, within arm's reach, sound asleep, all unaware. By God, how unaware of their own violent end the murdered always are! I tried to bring myself to act, but I couldn't. I even got as far as raising my arm, but then I let it fall by my side.

I thought of shutting my eyes and striking out blindly. It couldn't be done. To strike blindly is like not striking at all. And there's always the chance of stabbing the empty air. I had to strike with my eyes wide open, all five senses alert. And I had to keep calm, and regain the self-control that seemed to be leaving me now at the sight of my mother's body . . . Time went by and there I stood, motionless, still as a statue, unable to go through with the job. I didn't dare. After all, she was my mother, the woman who had borne me, a woman I had to spare if only for that reason . . . No, I shouldn't spare her on that account. She didn't do me any favor, no favor at all, bringing me into this world . . . There was no time to be lost. I would have to act once and for all. I was standing there like a sleepwalker, a knife in my hand, like a murderer in a wax museum . . . I struggled to overcome my paralysis, to pull myself together, to bring all my strength to bear. I was burning to get it done, quickly, and to run away, run until I fell down exhausted somewhere, anywhere. But I was wearing myself out standing there. I must have stood there an hour, stood there as if guarding her, as if watching over her dreams. Me, who had come to kill her, get rid of her, stab her to death!

I might have spent another hour this way. No, no, I must not. But I couldn't do what I had come to do either.

Perhaps another hour had already passed. No, I could not. It was beyond me, more than I had strength for, it sickened my blood. I thought of turning tail. But perhaps I would make a noise on the way out. She would wake up, recognize me, make me out in the gloom. No, I couldn't get away now, either. I was on the road to ruin . . . There was nothing for it but to strike out, strike, strike fast, and finish the job as fast as possible. But I couldn't strike, I couldn't raise my arm again . . . I seemed to be standing in a swamp, in the soft muck of a swamp, and sinking, gradually sinking, and no way out for me. I was up to my neck in the mud. I would drown like a cat . . . I couldn't kill, I couldn't move, I was paralyzed.

I turned slowly around to leave. The floor creaked. My mother shifted in her bed.

"Who's that?"

Now there really was no solution.

I threw myself upon her and held her down. She tried to free herself. At one point she had me by the throat. She shrieked like a woman in Hell. We fought. It was the most awful struggle you can imagine. We roared like wild beasts. We frothed at the mouth . . . In one round of the room I saw my wife, as white as a corpse, standing in the doorway, afraid to come in. She was holding a candle, and in its light I could see my mother's face, as purple as the robe of a Holy Week processionist . . . We grappled. My clothes were torn, my chest bare. The damned witch was stronger than a devil. I had to use all my strength to get her down. But every time I did, she slithered out of my grasp. She scratched me. She kicked me.

She hit me and bit me. Suddenly her mouth found my nipple, my left nipple, and tore it away. That was the moment I sank the blade into her throat . . .

Her blood spurted all over my face. It was warm as a soft belly and tasted like the blood of a lamb.

I dropped her and ran. Going out the door I collided with my wife and knocked her candle out. I took to the open, to the fields, cross country. I ran and ran without stopping, for a long time, for hours on end. The countryside was fresh-smelling, cool, and a sensation of great peace welled in my veins.

I could breathe . . .

ADDITIONAL NOTE BY
THE TRANSCRIBER

That is as far as the manuscript pages by Pascual Duarte go. Whether he went to the garrote shortly after writing these pages, or whether he had time to write of further feats in other pages now lost, is something I was never able to clear up.

Don Benigno Bonilla, the pharmacist in whose shop in Almendralejo I found, as I said before, the pages here transcribed, lent me all manner of help in my search. I turned the pharmacy inside out, like a sock. I rummaged in the porcelain jars, searched behind the bottles, above and below the cupboards, sifted the bicarbonate of soda. I learned some lovely names— Unguent of the Son of Zachariah, Oxherd and Coachman's Salve, Unguent of Rosin and Tar, of Pork Bread, of Laurel Leaves, of Charity, *and* Salve against Loose Bowels in Sheep. *The mustard made me cough, the valerian made me retch, the ammonia made me cry, but try as I might, and in spite of all the Our Fathers I offered up to St. Anthony, patron of lost objects, I never found what I was looking for, most likely because it probably did not exist.*

The total absence of any data concerning Pascual Duarte during his last years is a matter of no small frustration. It is not too difficult to calculate that he must have returned to

Chinchilla—we can infer as much from his own words. And there he must have remained until the year 1935, or perhaps even '36. In any case, it seems certain that he could not have been released from prison before the beginning of the Civil War. Since there is no human way of ascertaining the facts, we can add nothing about his activity during the fifteen days of revolutionary turmoil that swept over his village. Except for the killing of Don Jesús González de la Riva, Count of Torremejía—a deed of which our man was the confessed and convicted author—we know nothing, absolutely nothing, about Pascual Duarte in his later epoch; and even as regards this last crime we know only the stark irreparable fact, and nothing about his motives or the impulses which possessed him. For he was close-mouthed and talked only when the mood was upon him, which was seldom. Perhaps if his execution had been deferred, he might have reached that point in his memoirs and have gone into the event with some detail. But there was no stay of execution, and the only way we could fill the gap now would be to invent some fictional end, and that is something would ill befit the authenticity of this narrative.

Pascual Duarte's letter to Don Joaquín Barrera which I have placed at the beginning, must have been written at the same time as the chapters or sections which would be numbered XII and XIII had I numbered them. For these are the only two sections where he used a purple ink identical to that used in his letter to that gentleman. All of which goes to prove that Pascual did not, as he said he did, definitively suspend his story, but that instead he deliberately composed the letter so that it would have the maximum effect at the desired moment. This procedure shows our author to be scarcely as forgetful and vague as he seemed at first sight. One thing that is perfectly clear, for it is vouched for by a corporal of the Civil Guard, Cesáreo Martín, who carried out the request made of him by the prisoner, is the manner in which the bundle of manuscript papers were transferred from the Badajoz jail to the house of Señor Barrera in Mérida.

Anxious to throw as much light as possible on the last moments of Pascual, I wrote a letter to Don Santiago Lurueña, former prison chaplain, and now parish priest at Magacela (province of Badajoz), and another to Don Cesáreo Martín, formerly a private in the Civil Guard stationed in the Badajoz penitentiary and now corporal in command of the post at La Vecilla (province of León). In the pursuance of their duties both men were at Pascual Duarte's side when it came time for him to pay his debt to society.

Their letters to me follow.

I.

Magacela (province of Badajoz)
9 January, 1942

MY DEAR AND HONORED SIR:

I am just now in receipt of your kind letter of the 18th of December last, together with the 359 pages of typescript of the memoirs of the unfortunate Duarte, which reaches me after an evident delay. The whole package was forwarded to me by Don David Freire Angulo, the present chaplain of the Badajoz Prison and a classmate of your servant in our early seminary years at Salamanca. I wish to comply with the demands of conscience by writing these few words of acknowledgement immediately upon opening the envelope, leaving for tomorrow, God willing, the continuation of my letter, after I have read, following your instructions and to satisfy my own curiosity, the pages in front of me.

10 January

I have just read at one sitting—though Herodotus avows it to be a poor method—the confessions of Pascual Duarte. You have no idea of the profound impression they have made on my spirit, of the deep trace, the lasting furrow drawn in my soul. Your servant, who gathered Duarte's last words of repentance as joyfully as the farmer might garner a golden crop, could not help but be strongly moved by the written words of a man most people would consider a hyena (as I myself thought him when I was first summoned to his cell), though when the depths of his soul were probed it was easy to discover that he was more like a poor tame lamb, terrified and cornered by life.

His death was exemplary in its spiritual preparation. At the last moment, unfortunately, he lost his presence of mind. His will failed him and he was somewhat perturbed, with the results that the poor man suffered mental torture, where he might have saved himself this embarrassment had he possessed a whit more courage.

He disposed of his soul's business beforehand with an aplomb and serenity that left me astonished. In the presence of all and when the moment came to be led out into the yard he exclaimed: "May the Lord's will be done!" We were all amazed by his edifying humility. It was a shame that the Enemy should have robbed him of the glory of his last moments. Otherwise his death would certainly have been considered holy. But nevertheless he set an example for all who witnessed his end (until he lost control, as I said). Yet what I saw was fortunate in its consequences for me personally in my sweet ministry to afflicted souls. May the Lord have taken him into His holy bosom!

Believe me, sir, in the offer of the most sincere friendship of your humble

S. LUEREÑA, PRESBYTER

P.S. I regret I cannot oblige you in the matter of a photograph, nor do I know how to advise you to set about finding one.

That is the first letter, and here is the other.

II.

La Vecilla (Province of León),
1/12/42

MY DEAR SIR:

I hereby acknowledge receipt of your letter of December 18, and hope that the present communication finds you in the same good health you enjoyed when you wrote it. For my part I am well—thanks be to God—though stiffer than a board in this climate, which is not something to wish upon the greatest criminal. And now I will proceed to tell you about what you wish to know, for I see nothing to prevent me in the service regulations, though if there were anything against it, you would have to forgive me, since I would certainly not utter a single word. As for Pascual Duarte, the man you speak of, I certainly do remember him, for he was the most notorious prisoner that we guarded in many a day. I would not be able to vouch for the soundness of his mind, however, though you were to offer me the mines of Eldorado, for he did such things as clearly attested to his infirmity. Everything was all right until he once confessed. But the first time he did confess, apparently he was suddenly flooded with all kinds of remorse and scruples, and he decided to purge himself fully. In any case, the upshot was that on Mondays, because his mother or someone else was killed on that day, and on Tuesdays, because on Tuesday he had killed the Count of Torremejía, and on Wednesdays, because he had killed I don't know who, the unhappy wretch went half the week without a bite of food,

on a fast of his own making. In no time he had lost so much
weight that I began to wonder wouldn't the executioner have
an easy job making the two screws meet over his windpipe.
The poor devil spent all his days writing, as if he were in a
fever. But since he didn't bother anyone, and since the warden
was a kind-hearted man and had directed us to bring him
anything he needed in the way of writing supplies, we let him
alone and the fellow went at it with a will and never let up. He
trusted us, and one day he called me and showed me a letter
in an unsealed envelope (so I could read it myself, if I wanted
to, he told me), addressed to Don Joaquín Barrera López, in
Mérida, and he said to me in such a way that I could never
tell whether he was pleading with me or giving me an order:

"When they come to take me away, you put this letter in
your pocket, fix up this pile of papers here, and give everything to this gentleman. Do you understand?" And then he
said, looking into my eyes with such an air of mystery I was
really surprised:

"God will find a way to reward you . . . for I will ask Him
myself!"

I did what he wanted of me, for I saw nothing wrong in
it and because I have always been one to respect the wishes
of the dead.

As for his manner of dying, I will only tell you that it was
altogether undistinguished, a miserable death, and though
at first he strutted and declared in front of everyone "The
Lord's will be done!" which surprised us all considerably, he
soon forgot his bearing. At the sight of the scaffold he passed
out cold. When he came to again, he began to carry on so
about not wanting to die and its being a terrible thing to do
what they were doing to him, that he had to be dragged along
and put down on the stool by force. Finally he kissed a cru-
cifix held before him by Father Santiago, who was the prison

chaplain and a saint of a man. But he ended his days spitting and stamping, with no thought for the persons around him, in the most abject and the vilest way a man can die, letting everyone see his fear of death.

If at all possible, I should like to ask you to send me two copies of the book, rather than one, when it is printed. The other one is for the lieutenant of this sector, who tells me he will refund the price of the book by mail, if that is all right with you.

Trusting I have been of service to you, I remain, your humble servant,

CESÁREO MARTÍN

Your letter took some time to reach me, which is the reason for the delay between the two dates of our letters. It was forwarded to me from Badajoz, and I received it here on Saturday, the 10th, that is, the day before yesterday. Farewell.

What more can I add to the words of these two gentlemen?

Madrid, January, 1942

Printed in the USA
CPSIA information can be obtained
at www.ICGtesting.com
JSHW020747200923
48752JS00005B/6